# A PELICAN SWALLOWED MY HEAD

## AND OTHER ZOO STORIES

Written for the Wildlife Conservation Society
by Edward R. Ricciuti

SIMON & SCHUSTER BOOKS FOR YOUNG READERS
New York   London   Toronto   Sydney   Singapore

*In memory of Jerry Johnson, my friend and an Alabama farmboy who helped pioneer the modern zoo.*

SIMON & SCHUSTER BOOKS FOR YOUNG READERS
An imprint of Simon & Schuster Children's Publishing Division
1230 Avenue of the Americas, New York, New York 10020
Text copyright © 2002 by the Wildlife Conservation Society
Photographs copyright © 2002 by the Wildlife Conservation Society
SIMON & SCHUSTER BOOKS FOR YOUNG READERS is a trademark of Simon & Schuster.
Book design by Mark Siegel
The text of this book is set in GarthGraphic.
Printed in the United States of America
10 9 8 7 6 5 4 3 2 1
Library of Congress Cataloging-in-Publication Data
A Pelican Swallowed My Head and Other Zoo Stories/ written for the Wildlife Conservation Society by Edward R. Ricciuti.—1st ed.
p. cm.
ISBN 0-689-82532-3
1. Zoo animals—New York (State)—New York—Juvenile literature. 2. Zookeepers—New York (State)—New York—Juvenile literature. 3. New York Zoological Park—Juvenile literature. [1. Zoo animals. 2. Zookeepers. 3. New York Zoological Park. 4. Zoos.] I. Wildlife Conservation Society (New York, N.Y.) II. Title.
QL77.5 .R522 2001
590'.7'3747275—dc21                    00-052226

# INTRODUCTION

I magine if you could tour the entire world in a single day. One moment you are watching a polar bear in the frigid Arctic. The next, you are in the United States looking at a **beautiful monarch butterfly** flit among the flowers. A few minutes later you are in an African forest surrounded by gorillas of

every shape and size. As you continue to hop across the world you tour Europe, Asia, and Australia, and in each place you encounter one wondrous animal after another. Finally, at the end of your trip, you stand on the shores of the cold seas that stretch from southern South America to Antarctica. There you watch **penguins** rocket through the water and play in the icy waves. What an amazing adventure, and in a way it is possible

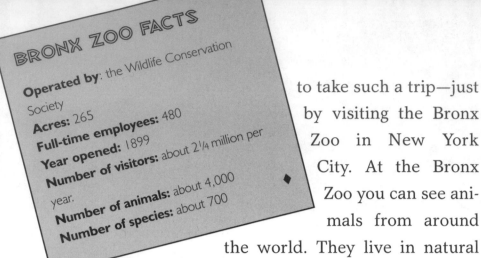

to take such a trip—just by visiting the Bronx Zoo in New York City. At the Bronx Zoo you can see animals from around the world. They live in natural habitats, full of plants, rocks, streams, and other natural features making their exhibits just like home. So in a way, visiting the Bronx Zoo is like seeing animals in wild places all over the globe.

Zoos have probably existed since the birth of civilization, and there are more than 150 accredited zoos—including aquariums, which are water zoos—in the United States and Canada. However, zoos today are different than they were in the past, when **animals were often kept in bare cages**. Back then animals were usually alone, without others of their kind to keep them company. They were probably bored, since they had nothing to do and no one to play with, and they couldn't have been happy **looking through steel bars** day after day. But since the 1960s, the Bronx Zoo has been a pioneer in changing the role of zoos by turning

them into conservation parks. Now the animals are in zoos not purely for people's entertainment—although, to be sure, going to a zoo is much more fun than ever. Zoo animals today work in their own way for environ-

mental conservation. **Kept in social groups of their own species** and combined with naturalistic surroundings, they are happier and healthier for it, as a result they behave much more naturally. Most importantly, especially for endangered species, they often reproduce young. One of a modern zoo's main functions is **to help disappearing species survive**. One way they do this is by breeding them in captivity. More than 80 percent of the mammals in today's zoos were born in

zoos. Unlike in the past, modern zoos seldom take animals from the wild, unless for a very good reason. For example, when an animal is in danger of extinction because its habitat is being destroyed, a zoo can be like a **modern Noah's ark**. Animals threatened with

extinction can be safeguarded in zoos and bred in hopes that, someday, they can be **released back into the wild.** For this to happen, however, their wild habitat must survive and the animals must be protected so they can rebuild their numbers.

Zoos also use animals to educate people about the importance of preserving wild animals and wild places. Thus, zoo animals have become modern-day ambassadors for the survival of their species in nature. Zoos hope that watching animals behaving naturally in modern

exhibits will inspire visitors to cherish wildlife. Zoo animals have so much to teach people about the wonders of the natural world and the fact that all of us depend on a healthy natural environment for our survival. ■

## WHO RUNS THE ZOO?

The Bronx Zoo is operated by an organization called the Wildlife Conservation Society. It was founded in 1895 as the New York Zoological Society. The society's headquarters are at the Bronx Zoo, however, that is not the only zoo under its banner. It operates three smaller zoos, also in New York City. And it operates an aquarium in New York City as well.

The work of the society, though, goes far beyond its zoos and aquarium. It has the world's leading international conservation program. Society scientists, researchers, and educators work in more than fifty countries to save endangered species and the ecosystems in which they live. These projects have ranged from helping the country of Belize, in Central America, to set up the first nature preserve for jaguars, to developing environmental education programs for youngsters in China. ◆

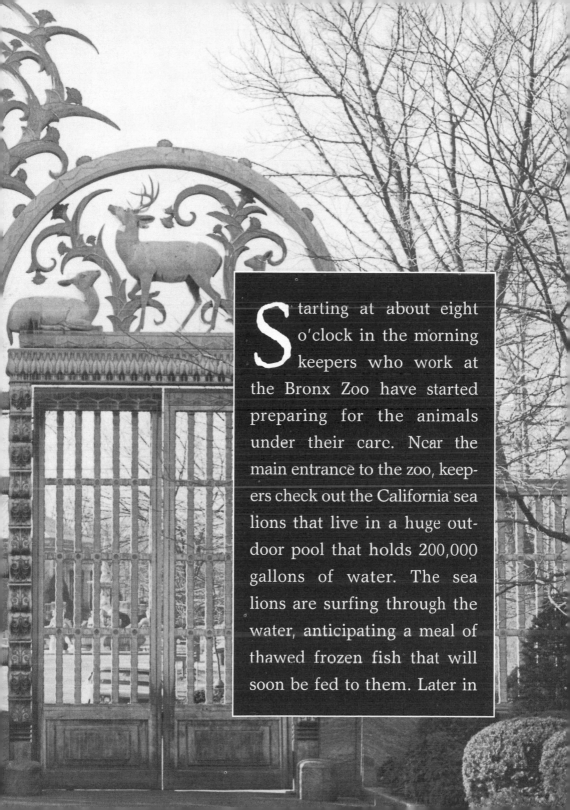

Starting at about eight o'clock in the morning keepers who work at the Bronx Zoo have started preparing for the animals under their carc. Ncar the main entrance to the zoo, keepers check out the California sea lions that live in a huge outdoor pool that holds 200,000 gallons of water. The sea lions are surfing through the water, anticipating a meal of thawed frozen fish that will soon be fed to them. Later in

a building called the World of Darkness, which houses exhibits for **nocturnal animals**, keepers have switched off the lights. The exhibits take on the appearance of a moonlit night, as huge bats—big as hawks and called flying foxes— rustle on their roosts. Pretty little leopard cats, the size of a house cat and spotted like a leopard, start to stir. They all have slept the night away. Their night, however, has been under lights, and now their day begins when the lights go off. Nocturnal animals sleep under the sun and are active under the moon. In the World of Darkness the day-night cycle on the outside of the building is reversed. The

animals living there snooze under bright lights when the zoo is closed and come out of hiding, in the artificial darkness, during the hours that visitors are in the building.

In another part of the zoo **Andean condors**, great horned owls, and **eagles** have awakened to the light of the real sun. They ruffle their feathers and blink their eyes in the morning light. These large birds live in individual exhibits within a large aviary. In a series of cages fronted by strings of vertical wire so fine that they are hardly visible, the birds behave much as they do in the wild. They have slept all night on perches that

have been erected for them in the exhibit, and within an hour or so keepers will enter the cages. They will keep a wary eye out, however, as these birds are large and fierce, and just because they have learned to tolerate their keepers, they are still wild animals. Going in to clean the exhibits and provide breakfast, the keepers serve each of the condors a nice fat rat for their morning meal. The rats have been frozen and then thawed a bit so the birds can eat them. Mmm! Yummy, don't you think?

## It's a Gorilla Good Morning

The Bronx Zoo's gorillas have spent the night snoozing in a private area behind their exhibit space. In the wild, gorillas sleep in nests that they make from branches and leaves, but at the zoo they rest in nests on shelves above the floor, covered with soft plant material such as hay. The wake-up call for the gorillas comes when the lights in their sleeping area are turned on. And then it's time to eat. "It's a good idea to let them sleep until the food is prepared," say the keepers. "If they wake up, they are like house cats that know it is time to eat and wait impatiently to be fed." And nobody wants to deal with an irritated gorilla that's hungry!

The gorillas receive some food outright—but other food items, such as peanuts, are hidden in various places within their exhibit. In the wild, gorillas naturally search for food, so in a zoo they can become bored if food is too easy to find. Gorillas like to keep busy, and poking around for food keeps them happy.

Another way to make gorillas happy is to give them things to do. In the wild, **gorillas regularly tear up shrubs and bushes,** all the while eating bits of leaves and bark. So each day, keepers provide the gorillas with all sorts of vegetation that has been cut on zoo grounds. Young and old, the gorillas play with the foliage, ripping it apart and tearing bark from the limbs as they eat it. Just like you and me, they like to have fun, so they dance around with the branches on their backs and roll around in the leaves. "They become totally involved," say the keepers. "They're obviously having fun and that's what we want. We like our gorillas to be happy."

## CURATORS, COLLECTION MANAGERS, AND KEEPERS — OH, MY!

Keeping zoo animals healthy and happy requires people with many different talents. Among the people who work at the Bronx Zoo are veterinarians, designers who develop exhibits, nutritionists, environmental educators, and members of the zoo's three animal departments.

In each of these departments—one for mammals, one for birds, and one for reptiles and amphibians—there is a curator. The term curator comes from the Latin word curare, which means "to care for." Below the curator are the collection managers. They are concerned with the overall management of the collection of animals in their depart-

ment. Then there are the keepers. They are the people who work most closely with the animals. They are also considered the zoo's front line, providing the

constant care that zoo animals require. Keepers prepare food and give it to the animals, clean their living quarters, and keep watch over them and their enclosures. Keepers must ask themselves a number of questions on a typical day: Does any animal look under the weather? Are all the water drains working? Are the animals getting enough to eat? Are they bored? But these are only a few of the things that a keeper has to think about. It is this sort of dedication on every level in every department that makes everything from morning feedings to reproduction programs run smoothly.

Working in a zoo sounds exciting, but it can also be like any other job: routine tasks to perform day after day; reports to be filed; equipment to be cleaned. However, zoo workers take great pleasure in working with their animals. They are extremely lucky, as they have something in their job that can't be found anywhere else—relationships with some of the most exotic and awe-inspiring creatures from all over the globe. ◆

The gorillas are allowed to enter the public viewing areas of the exhibit around 10 a.m., when the zoo opens to visitors. Before that keepers clean up the exhibit, providing the gorillas with new hay and hiding special treats like peanuts. But dragging hoses around and hauling bales of hay all day can be physically demanding, and not that long ago only men worked as zookeepers. But today more than half of the keepers are

women. The gorillas don't notice, though, and as long as they get their breakfast they're happy. Outsiders sometimes think that all zookeepers do is interact with animals. "What fun," they believe. But a good part of **a keeper's day involves some pretty tough labor**. It also takes a special love for animals.

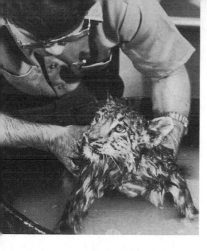

Some keepers simply like animals and want to help them, and some are fascinated by the diversity of animals and all the things they do. Other keepers are committed to environmental conservation and realize that by saving a species and its habitat, they can help save life on the planet. Whatever their attitude, one way or another, the people who care for zoo animals live out their dreams. **They get to know wild animals on a personal level,** and for gorilla keepers that means a constant commitment to the gorillas that are under their care.

The gorillas remain on exhibit until shortly after the zoo closes at 5 p.m., then they return to their sleeping area. The lights go out, and very likely, the keeper who shuts them down says to the gorillas, "Good night." And while that may be the end of the day for the gorillas, it isn't for the keepers. There is still a lot of cleaning up to do, as well as checking to make sure everything is secure for the night. When these last tasks are finished, the keepers can finally go home. Most, however, can't wait to come back to their gorillas the next morning. ■

**T**oday zoos around the world are devoted to saving species of animals that are in danger of extinction. Zoos like the Bronx Zoo are like modern versions of Noah's ark— places where animals that are in danger of becoming extinct can be preserved. In some cases zoos are the last really **safe sanctuaries** for animals that are disappearing from the wild. It is not enough, however, simply to protect animals that are rare or

# CHAPTER 2

# NOAH'S ARK

endangered. They must also be encouraged to reproduce. **That means babies, and lots of them!** But it also means that the female and male animals of the same breed must be introduced to

each other *and* get along well enough to mate. And just like people, animals sometimes don't get along, so this isn't always the easiest job.

# ENDANGERED AND THREATENED SPECIES

The United States Fish and Wildlife Service, which is part of the United States Department of the Interior, keeps a list of species that are in danger of extinction or are close to that point. Endangered species are on the brink of extinction. Threatened species are those that could become endangered in the near future. Below is the service's current list of major animal groups and the number of species in each group that are endangered or threatened:

**Mammals: 339**
**Birds: 274**
**Reptiles: 115**
**Amphibians: 27**
**Fish: 124**
**Clams: 71**
**Snails: 32**
**Insects: 43**
**Arachnids: 6**
**Crustaceans: 21**

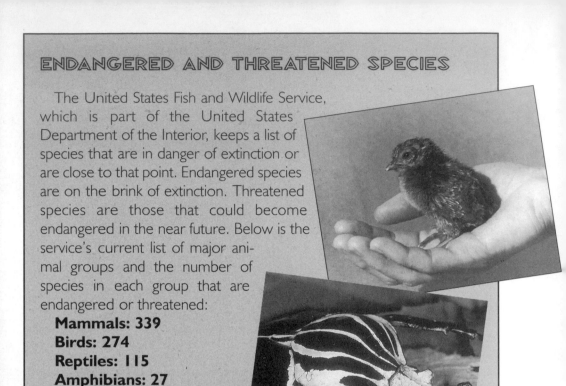

## Timmy

One day early in 1959 a female gorilla in the jungle of the West African country of Cameroon had a baby. It was a male, and like all young gorillas, he cuddled with his mother and, as time passed, became an adventurous toddler. He tried new foods—shoots and leaves of bamboo, for instance—and he played with other young gorillas. And sometimes, when he wanted attention, he pestered his mother and the other gorillas in his troop. But this little gorilla didn't romp in the tropical forest for very long—he was eventually captured and transferred to a zoo thousands of miles away. He was also given a new name: Timmy. Years later Timmy would become famous the world over, the

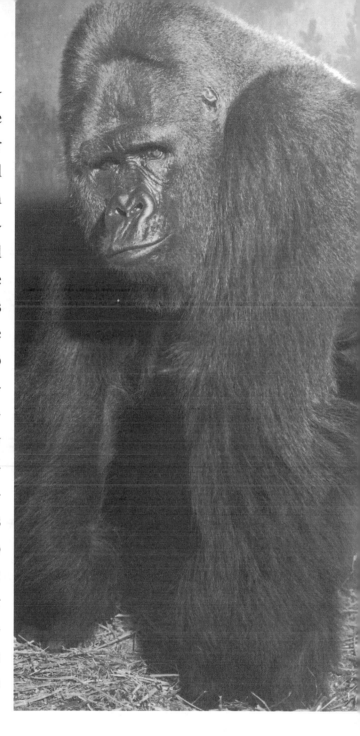

center of a huge controversy. He would also father several youngsters, helping his species, in the fight against extinction.

During the 1960s Timmy was living at Cleveland Metroparks Zoo, where he would stay for more than twenty-five years. He was always indoors and alone for the most part, but the Metroparks Zoo twice tried to give Timmy company by introducing him to female gorillas. The zoo hoped that Timmy would mate with them and together they would have a baby. North American zoos have cooperative programs for breeding rare animals such as gorillas, and about twenty gorillas are born each year. Timmy *was* interested in female company, but neither female responded to his affections, so in the late 1980s, the Metroparks Zoo tried again to provide Timmy with a mate. A female gorilla named Kate was sent to Cleveland from the zoo in Kansas City, Missouri, and was placed in Timmy's enclosure. Luckily, this time it worked. Timmy and Kate got along beautifully, but Kate never became pregnant. In 1990, the committee on gorillas among cooperating zoos eventually recommended that Timmy be sent to the Bronx Zoo, which had been chosen because of its success in breeding gorillas. It also had five females of breeding age who might be perfect for Timmy.

## PRICELESS PRIMATES

Timmy belongs to one of three types of gorillas that live in tropical Africa. He is a western lowland gorilla. They live in the deep forests of central and western Africa. Forests more to the east are the home of the eastern lowland gorilla, and even farther east there are gorillas living high in the cool wet mountain forests, known as mountain gorillas. All of these gorillas are in danger of extinction, mainly because their habitats are being destroyed by human activities such as farming and logging. Some African countries, however, are now thinking of gorillas as treasures—marvelous creatures that live nowhere else—and they have found that people from the outside will pay to come and see them. These great apes in the wild have now become tourist attractions, and the money from visitors helps pay to keep gorilla habitats safe in parks and preserves. ♦

In June 1991 the Metroparks Zoo announced that it was shipping Timmy to the Bronx. A few stories about Timmy's planned move appeared in Cleveland newspapers, but nobody paid much attention. A few weeks before Timmy was supposed to leave, however, a letter written by someone who purported that the author was Timmy was sent to area newspapers. The letter claimed that Timmy was frightened about the move and was in love with Kate, and if they were separated, he would be devastated. Newspeople laughed off the letter. "Sure a gorilla wrote the letter," said one newsman. "Like pigs have wings." And the story about Timmy's going to a new home seemed forgotten.

However, some Cleveland residents, especially animal activists, were very upset about the separation of Timmy and Kate. They believed that Timmy would never adjust to a new home after so many years in Cleveland, and that he had found the love of his life and should remain with her. Scientific knowledge about gorillas, though, said differently. Male and female gorillas do not become attached for life, and they may have many different mates. The animal activists disagreed, and the city's parks board received a petition from more than five hundred people demanding that Timmy stay in Cleveland. This triggered new interest in the story by the media, and suddenly Timmy was making headlines throughout the United States as well as overseas. Meanwhile, animal rights groups went to court, asking a judge to stop Timmy's move, but on October 31 the judge ruled that Timmy should be transferred to the Bronx.

Since it was Halloween, kids were trick-or-treating all over the country as Timmy made his way to New York. He was housed in a large crate, carried inside a van that was one of several vehicles in a long caravan. Along for the ride were a mammal keeper from the Bronx Zoo, two keepers, two veterinarians, and the curator of mammals from the Cleveland zoo. Everyone took turns riding in the cargo space with Timmy to keep him company.

As the caravan sped through the night Timmy and his friends were escorted by state police cruisers, their lights flashing in the darkness. Other motorists on the road might well have wondered if an important person was headed somewhere, guarded by police. If they did, they were not far off. Timmy had become quite a celebrity.

The reason for the police escort, however, was fear that animal rights extremists might cause trouble along the way. Nothing ever happened, but back in Cleveland there were loud objections. Protesters marched in front of the zoo and carried signs with messages such as "Timmy is Cleveland's own. So, bring him home" and "Tax dollars support suffering." And though they might have had the best of intentions, they weren't working in the best interests of Timmy and his species.

When Timmy arrived at the Bronx Zoo, he was placed in a quarantine enclosure within the zoo's **Great Apes House** and kept there for a month. This is

standard procedure for animals new to the zoo. They are kept in quarantine to make sure that they are healthy and ready for their new home, and it also gives them a chance to rest and adjust to their new surroundings. While in quarantine Timmy also got to know the people who would care for him. "He settled in quite well," says James G. Doherty, the zoo's general curator. "We were very pleased with how he adjusted to his new home and new people." It wasn't long before Timmy went to a holding area adjacent to other gorillas in the Great Apes House, where he was kept in a large enclosure and given toys, like burlap bags and cardboard boxes, to play with. He was still indoors, but eventually that would change. Zoo staff members carefully observed Timmy's behavior and personality, and once they believed that he was comfortable in his new home, they decided to introduce him to a few female gorillas they thought would be a good match. Usually gorillas new to one another are placed in an enclosure together for only a few minutes or hours, and then the time is gradually extended. If things go smoothly, they are soon left together all the time. No one was sure what would happen with Timmy.

Inside the Great Apes House's off-exhibit quarters Timmy was getting acquainted with his prospective mates, and little by little, throughout the winter, he got to know them. He seemed most comfortable with **Pattycake**, a nineteen-year-old female. Timmy also seemed to get along with two other female gorillas named Tunko and Julia. And after a life that had for the most part been quite lonely, Timmy finally had friends with which to socialize, an important factor if gorillas are to be happy.

By May, Timmy was ready for a major step—a step into the outdoors. The zoo was planning on putting Timmy in a brand-new enclosure, and for the first time since he had been taken from his native Africa, Timmy would be able to walk in the open. He would be able to feel the breeze and see it flutter leaves on the trees. Timmy's coming-out party was held in the gorilla habitat on the outside of the Apes House. First Pattycake, Julia, and Tunko were released into the outside enclosure. For them it was familiar territory, so they were perfectly at ease, but Timmy was not so sure. When the door to the outside area opened, he looked somewhat uncertain. His deep-set eyes surveyed the unknown territory ahead, and his nostrils quivered as he took in the unfamiliar smells. No one could read Timmy's mind, but perhaps he was a little scared. His huge head poked out of the Great Apes House door, and walking in typical gorilla fashion, with his knuckles on the ground, he edged out of the building. Things did not go far, however; Timmy simply sat on a large flat rock near the building's wall and looked around.

The bonds that Timmy had established with Pattycake, Julia, and Tunko over the last few months had become powerful. As they played in the grass Timmy looked at them, and they watched him, their eyes warm with interest. Their familiarity with the area may have reassured him that he was safe. In effect, they were asking him to come out and play. As

Timmy eventually got up to approach the females he seemed uncertain about something. Zoo staffers who were observing his every move finally realized what it was: grass. Timmy was not used to the feel of grass. He had apparently forgotten the forest world in which he was born, where living vegetation had surrounded him. Clearly he was apprehensive, but the attraction of his friends was very strong, and as Timmy finally moved toward them they gathered around him in welcome. At thirty-three years of age, Timmy had friends and he had begun a new life.

But Timmy's zoo story wasn't over by a long shot. The hair on his back was growing increasingly tinged with gray—he was becoming a silverback, a male gorilla in his prime. Shortly after going outside for the first time, Timmy was observed mating with Pattycake, and on July 11, she gave birth to a baby, a male gorilla weighing five and a half pounds that was named **Okpara**. Since then Timmy has fathered twelve other youngsters,

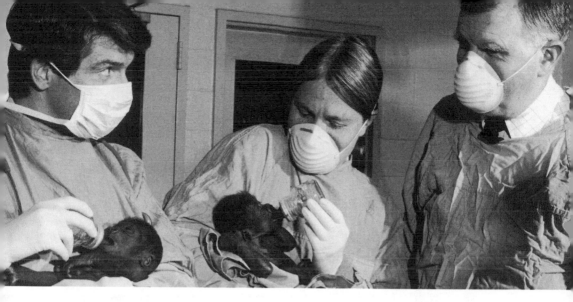

including **a rarely seen set of twins**, and he is now the leader of his own troop of more than a dozen gorillas. Zoo staffers marvel at how caring Timmy is as a father and a leader. "He's wonderful," says senior keeper

Denise Smith. "**He's the most perfect silverback you could have**. When the troop leaves its sleeping area for the day, he waits until they all go out. He keeps track of each and every one of them. He plays with the babies, holding and tickling them, and he makes sure the older youngsters don't play too roughly with the younger ones."

Timmy is clearly one content gorilla, and in being so, he is helping preserve his own species. One day, perhaps, some of his descendants may be released into the African forest, where he first breathed the air and saw the light of day. But that day is still far off.

These breeding programs are aimed at increasing the numbers of endangered animals in captivity in order to release them into the wild someday. But if this is to happen, wild areas must be preserved. This is why the Bronx Zoo, and other zoos, spend vast amounts of time and money to help preserve wilderness areas around the globe. Breeding rare animals such as gorillas and returning them to the wild is not a new idea, but the Bronx Zoo was one of the first zoos to try it. Only a few years after the Bronx Zoo opened, it pioneered the technique of reintroducing animals into the wild.

## Return of the Bison

On December 1, 1905, fifteen men and one woman gathered for a meeting in the Lion House at the Bronx Zoo. They included scientists, sportsmen, and businesspeople. Among them were William T. Hornaday, the first director of the Bronx Zoo; Edward Cave, editor of *Field & Stream* magazine; Martin Schenck, the chief engineer of the Bronx parks department; and Charles H. Townsend, director of the New York Aquarium. United States President Theodore Roosevelt,

who was a passionate outdoorsman and a talented nature writer, was not there, but he was aware of the meeting—and very interested in its outcome.

The reason for the meeting was the American buffalo, or bison. A century before, sixty million bison had roamed the plains of western North America. They were by far the most numerous large mammals on the continent, perhaps anywhere in the world. **Native American tribes of the Great Plains relied on them for food.** But by the 1880s wild bison were almost extinct. They had been victims of a horrifying slaughter. Hordes of "buffalo hunters" had invaded the plains, wiping out herd after herd, skinning the dead animals for their valuable hides and leaving their car-

casses to rot. The United States government had shamefully encouraged the killing, as it was a way of solving the "Indian problem," as it was called at the time. Without bison the Great Plains tribes would starve, and the only way they could survive would be to settle on government reservations. An ugly time in American history, no doubt. By the turn of the century the only sizable herd of wild bison were a few hundred living in Canada. There were about twenty in Yellowstone National Park, but they were hardly wild, as the game wardens protected and fed them. There were also several small herds being kept by private citizens, and a few of the shaggy beasts remained in zoos, including the Bronx Zoo. The bison in captive herds were reproducing young as successfully as they did in nature, so there was some insurance against the creature falling over the brink of extinction. The meeting in the zoo's Lion House was the beginning of the American Bison Society. Its goal was to reestablish herds of wild bison in the West.

Roosevelt supported the society with the full weight of his presidency, and in October 1907 he wrote the organization a letter: "I feel real and great interest in the work being done by the American Bison Society to preserve the buffalo—the biggest of the American big game. . . . It would be a misfortune to permit the species to become extinct."

The American Bison Society began working with the United States government to establish herds of bison, gathered from private collections, in new preserves out west. Among the first captive bison to be shipped to these preserves came from the Bronx Zoo. This was the beginning of what would be a very successful program, and today American bison again roam many areas of the West. Most of them are on federal lands, such as national parks, and on Native American reservations. The great herds that shook the prairies with their passing are gone, but the bison as a species is no longer in danger of vanishing, and they again roam wild and free.

## Mad Max

His official name is Max, but keepers at the Bronx Zoo also call him Mad Max. He is an okapi, **a rare relative of the giraffe.** Unlike giraffes, which live on open African plains, okapis inhabit the shadowed, dense tropical forests of central Africa. Max was born in a

German zoo on October 19, 1972. He is the oldest okapi in captivity, and quite possibly, in the world, as many zoo animals usually live longer than their relatives in the wild. The breeding program for okapis is an important part of efforts to save this rare species. The okapi seems to have never been very common, as it lives only in the Ituri Forest of Democratic Republic of Congo (DRC), formerly Zaire, which is considered one of the most impenetrable wildernesses on Earth. But even this dense forest is slowly being damaged by the logging trade and the creation of roads. The okapi, shy and wary, needs an undisturbed habitat.

But Max has lived in several zoos during his lifetime. He has also been used in a number of breeding programs to increase the number of okapis in zoos. In fact, three calves at the Bronx Zoo call him their dad.

So remote is the forest inhabited by the okapi that this large animal was not discovered by foreigners until 1901. Explorers in DRC sent two pieces of okapi hide to scientists in London for identification. At first scientists believed that the okapi was a member of the horse family, but when they eventually compared the skulls of an okapi and a giraffe, they realized the two animals were related.

Max arrived at the Bronx Zoo in 1992 and now lives in a building called the Carter Giraffe Building, which also houses Baringo giraffes, rare Grevy's zebras, and endangered cheetahs. But while zoo visitors can see other okapis, they never get a glimpse of Max. He is there for breeding purposes only and is kept off exhibit. Next door is an enclosure where another okapi, named Kuamba, lives. Kuamba is a female that mates with Max during breeding season. She can be seen with whatever calf she has at the time, and although Max can see them, whether they are there or not probably

makes no difference to him. In the wild adult okapis are true loners. They stay by themselves, moving through the forest like ghosts; only during the breeding season do males and females get together.

Max is known as Mad Max because he can be grouchy. "He isn't really friendly," says senior keeper Kristine Theis. "The other okapis like to be petted, but not Max." She does admit, however, that when she stands in front of his stall, he sometimes licks her across the forehead. Max is most grouchy when he is with a female for breeding. "Then," says Kristine, "he can be very difficult." When keepers enter the breeding enclosure, Max often charges them. "He runs right at you," says Kristine. The charge, however, is just a bluff, because Max always comes to a halt and then goes back to the female. So even though he can be feisty, keepers have quite a great affection for this wild guy. After all, he is a real old-timer who continues to conserve and increase the number of his species.

## Animal Attraction

Gorillas Timmy and Pattycake hit it off rather quickly when they met, but perhaps no two animals at the Bronx Zoo have ever paired off so rapidly as **two eclectus parrots** once did. These parrots, which come from Australia, New Guinea, and the Solomon Islands, are peculiar in that the male and female look like two

entirely different species of birds. The male is emerald green, while the female has not one green feather on her body. She may be red, blue, or purple. Some people think that these birds are the most beautiful of all parrots, but sadly these wondrous birds are dwindling in the wild, and as their numbers decrease, zoos and parrot breeders are fighting to raise them in captivity.

A few years ago a woman who owned a female eclectus parrot as a pet telephoned the Bronx Zoo's Bird Department. "I can't keep my bird any longer," she said. "Will you take it?" This may sound odd, but her case was not unusual. Many people who buy parrots for pets find they have made the wrong decision. Parrots can be noisy, destructive, and very messy—but most of all, they demand lots of attention and companionship. People sometimes find that they have underestimated the time and effort required to care for a parrot, so they try to find a new home for their pet, often by calling zoos. But unfortunately zoos cannot take every parrot that is offered to them.

This particular parrot offered to the Bronx Zoo was another matter, however. Because the bird was so rare, the zoo told the woman that the bird was welcome. When the parrot arrived, it was in a cage only two feet square, which is hardly enough room for a bird that stands fourteen inches high. Yet it had lived in the cage for seven years, so when keepers tried to remove it from its cramped quarters, they found that they had a problem. The parrot seemed terrified. "It climbed the walls of the cage and screamed," says Donald Bruning, curator and chairman of the Bird Department.

For a month the bird was kept under quarantine. Keepers watched it carefully. "Everybody was convinced that it was a psycho," says Don, but it turned out that that opinion was far from the truth. After the quarantine period keepers hauled the cage containing the parrot to a holding area in the World of Birds building. There they placed the parrot's cage inside a larger flight cage—eight feet high, six feet wide, and seven feet long. "We tied the door to the parrot's cage open," says Don, "and put some food just outside it." Don and his keepers left the flight cage and watched, hopefully, but the parrot stayed put. "For three months, the most she did was put her head out of her cage to grab some food. She looked hopeless," he remembers.

Then the zoo received a male eclectus parrot on loan from a breeder. The male was placed in another flight cage next to the one where the female was housed, and by the next day the male parrot had obviously worked some sort of parrot magic. When keepers went to the flight cage area, they saw that the female had not only left her small cage, but had climbed the wall of the flight cage. And perched up at the top with her was the male who had ascended the wire of his cage to be next to her. They were so close that they could touch bills, and they were actually exchanging bits of food. "That means they were courting, as if preparing to breed," Don explains. "We were astounded."

The two birds were placed together, and before long they had a baby chick—and following that, several more. Eventually they were sent to a facility in Florida that specializes in breeding parrots, so to continue reproducing their own kind. "That female taught us all a lesson," says Don. "Never say that anything is hopeless."

## Angel and Mrs. McNasty

Sometimes relations between the sexes are not so smooth. Several years ago there was a female Andean condor at the zoo whose memory still makes Bird Department keepers quake in their work boots. She was, in a word, AWFUL. So much so that she was nicknamed Mrs. McNasty.

"She was the nastiest condor that I've ever met," says Eric Edler, a Bronx Zoo veteran who is collection manager for the department—and a nasty condor can be a terror. **The Andean condor is the world's largest flying bird,** weighing up to thirty pounds, with a wingspan of about ten feet. Native to South America, it feeds largely on the remains of dead animals, which it tears to shreds with its wicked, hooked beak.

Mrs. McNasty lived in the zoo's eagle aviary, which is a series of huge flight cages containing vegetation and tree limbs that serve as perches. Inside lived various sorts of eagles, owls, and other vultures, of which the condor was one. But Mrs. M seemed unable to get along with anyone, human or bird. "She would walk up to keepers and act very friendly," says Eric. "But it really was just an act." Given a chance, Mrs. McNasty would strike, and once she slashed a keeper so viciously in the arm with her bill that the keeper needed thirty stitches.

She was even nastier to other condors. When a new female was placed in the aviary with her, Mrs. McNasty grabbed it by the head with her bill. "She shoved that bird's head under water in a drinking container," says Eric, "and a keeper had to pull her off."

Everyone knew that Mrs. McNasty wasn't friendly, but the big question was whether she could ever be matched with a male. The general consensus was

"Forget about it," and since the zoo was trying to raise condors for release in the South American country of Peru, it was becoming a big problem. The keepers knew it was going to be difficult, but they kept thinking. Surely there had to be a male condor out there that could turn this feathered furor into a lovebird.

Eventually the Bird Department discovered **Angel, a male condor** that was a relatively easygoing bird, and thought they might get along. And miraculously, for some unknown reason, they did. Angel and Mrs. M mated and produced several eggs, most of which were hatched in an incubator because the keepers weren't sure if the Mrs. would take care of them. Everything seemed to be going well, but then Mrs. McNasty seemed to tire of Angel. She started beating up on him—his charm had apparently faded. Mrs. McNasty is now long gone, and Angel, a much younger condor, still remains at the zoo. One wonders though, if condors can remember, does Angel think of Mrs. McNasty with fondness or fear?     ■

# CHAPTER 3
# FAMILY TIES

G rowing up in a family, as young gorillas do, is not something that all animals experience. In fact, most animals are on their own from their first moment of life. Codfish, for example, hatch from eggs left floating in the sea by their mother, and she has nothing else to do with them, except perhaps to eat them if she encounters them again. The female boa constrictor, on the other hand, bears her young alive, but once they are born, they are totally on their own. Many animals, however, have **strong family ties**. This is particularly true of mammals, whose family life is the most developed in the animal kingdom. In mammal families, such as those of gorillas and wolves,

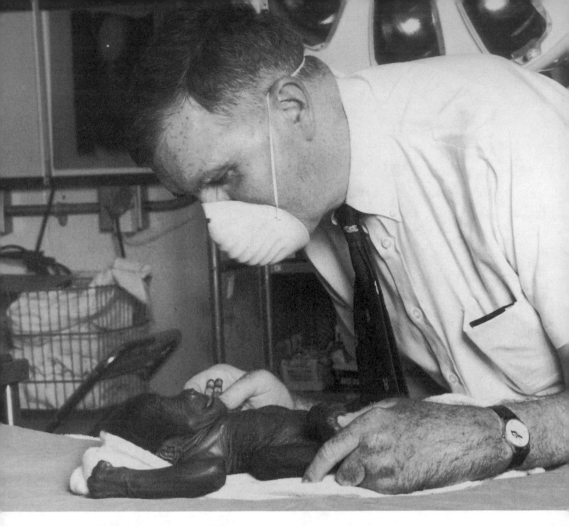

both male and female parents care for their young.
Other adults in the community lend a hand too. In the
case of wildcats the mother is the only one responsible
for the young. After mating, the male goes his own
way, leaving the female to give birth and raise her
young. And if you have ever had a house cat that has
had a litter of kittens, you've probably noticed that

female cats are excellent mothers. This sort of under-standing is an integral part of Bronx Zoo animal staffers' jobs. After all, a major part of their mission is **to ensure that young zoo animals grow into healthy adults**. And it's these staffers who know when certain animals should be left alone to rear their young, and when others, like some gorillas, need a hand. In the latter situation the keepers end up becoming part of the family.

For example, in the wild, gorillas live in troops of up to a few dozen animals. The troop is headed by a silver-back, which is a male gorilla in his prime. Often the only male in the troop that breeds, he watches over the rest of the troop, which consists of subadult males and females, juveniles from three to six years old, and infants. The gestation period of gorillas is two weeks less than that of humans, so newborn gorillas are as helpless as human babies; however, baby gorillas develop twice as fast. They cannot hold on to their mothers alone at first, but when they get a few months older, they hang on for piggyback rides as their mothers jump from tree to tree. They are eating solid food at around three months and are walking after only four.

The baby gorilla can nurse for up to a year, and if the mother is unable to do so, the zoo must step in.

Starting in 1972, when the first gorilla was born at the zoo, babies have been raised by surrogate mothers in the zoo nursery. Females are sometimes unsure how to raise infants, and so the zoo doesn't take any chances, as under a staffer's care their condition can easily be monitored. Actually, a baby gorilla has a better chance of surviving in a zoo than in the wild. And just like human babies, they sleep in cribs and drink milk from baby bottles. As gorilla exhibits have improved— and zoo people have learned more about these apes— an increasing number of mothers have begun to rear their own young, which is ultimately the best for both the baby and the zoo.

## Little Big Mama

Perhaps the most unusual animal family at the Bronx Zoo is that of a tiny mammal with a really weird name: **the naked mole-rat**. This little creature is between three and five inches long and weighs only a few ounces. Like its name, the naked mole-rat is most definitely naked and looks like a cross between a mole and a rat. Its wrinkly pink skin is bare except for a handful

of whiskerlike hairs, scattered here and there over the surface. However, it is *not* a rat. *Nor* is it a mole. But it is a rodent, as are rats and moles. Actually, a naked mole-rat looks very much like a real newborn rat, which is hairless and pinkish gray. Like moles, naked mole-rats live underground in tunnels and have small, squinty eyes, which make them virtually blind. This is of no matter, as vision is practically useless in the underground darkness. Instead of seeing, naked mole-rats feel their way around with the hairs on their bodies. Their bare skin is also an advantage underground, as it enables them to slide through tight tunnels with ease. The naked mole-rat may have tiny eyes, but it has huge front teeth. Two on top and two on the bottom, these teeth are so big that they resemble tusks, like those of

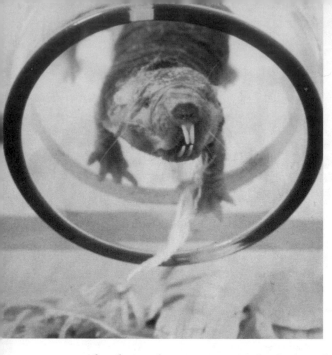

a walrus. In fact, *Wildlife Conservation* magazine has described naked mole-rats as "wrinkled and tusked, resembling nothing quite so much as tiny walruses from outer space." Space creatures or not, naked mole-rats use their **walrus-like teeth** to dig their tunnels and to gather food. Their diet consists mostly of tubers, which are similar to potatoes and can be found growing off underground roots.

Like its oddball name and bizarre appearance, the naked mole-rat's family life is extraordinary for a mammal. The naked mole-rat family actually has more in common with those of ants and bees than any other animals. Like these insects, naked mole-rats live in colonies. Only one female in the colony, which can number from a few dozen to hundreds of animals, bears young. As in a bee or ant colony, she is called the queen, and only a handful of males mate with her.

Most other colony members are workers, who dig tunnels, clean, and supply the colony with food. But where do these strange animals come from?

Back in 1842 a German scientist working in East Africa kept running across small, low cones of earth scattered about the desert. Curious as to what they were, he dug up some of them, and below each cone he found a network of tunnels and chambers, some reaching more than six feet below the surface. These underground mazes swarmed with strange little creatures that the scientist had never seen before, and apparently no other scientist had ever reported this species of mammal. Soon thereafter the naked mole-rat became known the world over. But even though naked mole-rats were discovered years ago, it wasn't until recently that zoos exhibited them. Then, during the 1990s a handful of zoos opened naked mole-rat exhibits, one of them at the Bronx Zoo.

The Bronx Zoo's naked mole-rat exhibit is in a building called the World of Darkness. It contains exhibits of animals that are active at night, as well as creatures that live underground. The naked mole-rat exhibit gives visitors a close-up view of the creatures' underground city. Visitors can peer into it through cut-away sections and even watch the mole-rats on a tele-vision monitor, so they can observe the everyday life of the colony. The nests that naked mole-rats dig are very complex and are comprised of **tunnels, nurseries, feeding chambers, and even toilets**.

Since all the young in a colony of naked mole-rats

come from the queen, they are all brothers and sisters, or half brothers and half sisters. So when a zoo decides to exhibit naked mole-rats, it cannot simply put a bunch of unrelated animals together. The result would be chaos. A full colony—or, at least, a group of mole-rats taken from one colony already in existence—must be placed in the exhibit from the very beginning. The colony at the Bronx Zoo was sent there by a scientist in Africa and at first count contained twenty-three animals. Zoo staffers named its queen, Mary, and like other naked mole-rat queens, Mary was truly a little big mama. A queen is about twice the weight of the others in the colony, growing up to nine inches long. This is another way in which mole-rats resemble bees and ants, as queen bees and ants are also much larger than the rest of their colonies. A naked mole-rat queen can have a litter of up to twenty or more young every eighty days, and that makes for lots of mole-rat "pups," as they are called, to fill the nurseries. During Mary's lifetime at the zoo she had more than four hundred pups, some of which were eventually placed in a second mole-rat city, next to Mary's colony. Others were removed from the exhibit and used to start new colonies held in reserve, behind the scenes. Generally, no more than one hundred naked mole-rats are on exhibit, although, mammal curator Pat Thomas says, "It's hard for us to tell exactly how many because we don't like to disturb the colony and handle them."

In typical naked mole-rat fashion, Mary had her young in a nursery chamber, but while there, she had plenty of company. In a naked mole-rat colony there are several adults that never help out with routine work. However, they are not shirkers. They have an important role to play in colony life, and it has to do with making sure that the young stay warm. Since they are bare, naked mole-rats have a difficult time conserving their body heat the way other mammals do, but they generally stay warm enough to be comfortable. Temperatures underground are much more stable than at the surface, and in nature—as well as at the zoo—they usually stay around eighty degrees Fahrenheit. Even so, there are times when naked mole-rats, especially newborns, who are hardly more than an inch long at birth, feel a bit chilly. When that happens, they huddle up, sharing body warmth, and that is why the nonworkers are so important. They cluster around the pups to keep them warm and cozy. Like other young mammals, baby naked mole-rats live at first on their mother's milk, and later on they change to vegetable food, which is brought to them by workers— just as ants and bees feed the young in their colonies.

When not tending to her young, Queen Mary makes the rounds in her colony. Known for being a tough boss, if she finds a worker goofing off, she gives it a sound push with her nose, which is usually enough to make the lazy worker get busy again. But naked mole-rat queens can also be bullies. Scientists believe that other females in the colony do not mate because the queen prevents it by force, also to keep the colony from growing too large. So you might say that the queen mole-rat is definitely the "queen bee" of her colony.

Speaking of competition, when a naked mole-rat queen dies, other females in the colony compete for her crown. Sometimes they engage in fights, or they simply try to intimidate one another. Scientists are not sure how one female ultimately wins the struggle. "Not every female can be a queen," says Pat Thomas. "It may be just a case of which female grows bigger and stronger first." But like all queens, Mary eventually grew old and passed on, and Pat Thomas and other zoo staffers watched the colony to see what would happen. They were interested to find that there was little or no fighting among the contenders for the crown, and eventually a new queen emerged. As years pass there will be other new queens of the zoo's mole-rat colonies, but none will be as popular among the zoo staff as Mary. After all, she was the first.

## INSIDE THE NAKED CITY

Naked mole-rats not only have families like those of bees, but are as busy as bees. Workers regularly dig new tunnels, some of which can include more than two miles of tunnels, and individual workers often dig small tunnels on their own. When it comes to major construction projects, however, the workers operate as a well-organized team. They form a chain, one behind the other, that acts like a conveyor belt. At the head of the chain is a digger. This mole-rat loosens the soil with its tusks and pushes it backward mostly with its hind feet. The worker behind the digger is the mover, who continues to move the soil backward, crawling under the other workers in the chain. They, in turn, creep forward and, one after another, take turns behind digger. Meanwhile, when each mover reaches the rear of the chain, it turns its load of soil over to the worker that is near the surface. This mole-rat kicks loose earth upward through an opening, where it forms the low cones of soil that first prompted the curiosity of a certain German scientist many years ago. Every so often the digger and the mole-rat that creates the cones are relieved by other members of the work party and then take their turns as movers.

When they're not digging, naked mole-rats roam their tunnels in search of tubers. When one of them finds some, it bites off a hunk and brings it back to the colony. Other mole-rats can retrace its steps by following its scent and head for the food source. This is another way the behavior of naked mole-rats is surprisingly similar to that of ants. They, too, follow one another to food by means of scent trails. ♦

## Ivy and Snow Prince

**Snow leopards** live high in the cold mountains of central Asia and are considered by some to be the most beautiful of the big cats. Their fur, adapted for cold conditions, is thick and long and is silvery gray with elegant black markings. But this gray ghost of the mountains no longer roams many of the areas where it was once found. Snow leopards are in danger of extinction, and only a few thousand of them remain in the wild. For many years zoos around the world desperately tried to breed snow leopards in captivity with no success. And it wasn't until the 1960s, that a zoo in Copenhagen, Denmark achieved the goal. Having succeeded at such a miraculous birth, they eventually sent along one of their male snow leopards to the Bronx Zoo for breeding. His name was Bowser II, and after a few years he fathered the Bronx's first baby snow leopard. The mother was a wild-caught female named Miss Bronx Zoo, and since then the Bronx Zoo has been breeding snow leopards on a regular basis.

Ivy was born at a zoo in what used to be East Germany, and was sent to the Bronx in 1992. She

was very special because one of her parents had been taken from the wild, and since many of the snow leopards in United States zoos are related, inbreeding is a constant threat. The Bronx Zoo staffers knew that if Ivy produced a cub, she would inject new, wild blood into their snow leopard collection. Ivy eventually mated with Bach, a Bronx Zoo male, and early on a June morning gave birth to a single cub in a quiet maternity room with two chambers. They named him Snow Prince. "We had to watch [Ivy] carefully but did not want to disturb her in the beginning," says senior keeper Marty Zyburu, "so we used a video camera." Keepers not only watched Ivy and Snow Prince on a monitor, but painstakingly reviewed videotapes of their nighttime activities every day. They carefully observed how Ivy reacted to her youngster. "She seemed to have a feel for mothering," says Marty. Marty and his keepers watched Snow Prince snuggle up to his mother and nurse as Ivy licked her cub affectionately. Ivy might have been a brand-new mother, but she didn't act like it. "We really didn't have any problems," says Marty, "she went through it pretty well."

After a week keepers separated Snow Prince from his mother, and zoo veterinarians gave the cub a thorough health check, which they continued to do every few weeks as he grew older. As Snow Prince continued to grow, he became increasingly energetic. He would stalk his mother's bushy tail with his small body close to the ground, then he would launch himself up and pounce on it. It didn't seem to bother Ivy, as she knew Snow Prince was playing, but he was also learning. Stalking and pouncing are techniques that snow leopards use to catch prey in the wild. **Snow Prince eventually grew into a healthy young snow leopard,** and because he was only two generations removed from the wild, he was more than a prince—he was a prize. As for Marty and the keepers who have watched Snow Prince grow up, they are quite proud of him and themselves. Their hard work and dedication have helped another endangered species along in its fight for survival.

## MOTHER'S LITTLE HELPERS

**Tamarins** are tiny monkeys from South America that are so small when they are babies they can sit on your finger. Not surprisingly, baby tamarins require lots of extra care. But not to worry, as they get lots of attention not only from their mother and father, but also from their older brothers and sisters. In fact, big brothers and sisters let the babies ride on their backs, as their father and mother do. They also help keep them clean, but at the end of the day it's the mother that rules the roost. According to mammals supervisor Kim Tropea, one of the best mother tamarins at the Bronx Zoo was Binky. She had twenty babies and, with the help of the rest of the family, cared for them so well that not a single one was lost. But Binky and her brood were also very demanding. "If we were a few minutes late at feeding time, they would screech at us," Kim says. "We would come into the cage and they would gather around us, yelling, so we fed them right away." But you can't blame Binky or her family for the racket; they clearly knew whose job was whose.  ♦

## Norma, Sasha, and Alexis

About three months before Snow Prince was born, another big cat gave birth for the first time. Her name is Norma and she is a **Siberian tiger** who lives in the section of the zoo called Wild Asia. Here she and other tigers are exhibited outdoors and viewed by visitors riding a monorail called the Bengali Express. The tigers

can be seen in the outdoors year-round, and since they come from parts of northern Asia where winters bring blizzards and temperatures far below zero, New York City winters are hardly a problem. Siberian tigers are the biggest of all tigers, and some of them weigh more than six hundred pounds. Like snow leopards, Siberian tigers are in danger of extinction. There are probably fewer than three hundred of them remaining in the wild, and not surprisingly, many zoos around the world are breeding these beautiful big cats. In fact, more Siberian tigers now live in zoos than in nature, and **every time a Siberian tiger is born in a zoo, it is**

**cause for celebration**. But when Norma gave birth, there was a double celebration because she had twins—Sasha, a male, and Alexis, a female.

Chris Wilgenkamp, who is the head of the Wild Asia keepers, arrived at his small office early on the morning of March 7, 1997, knowing that Norma was ready to give birth. She had been resting in the seclusion of a wooden birthing box, and as Chris entered the office he immediately went to a video monitor that was connected to a camera inside the box. What he saw made him very happy: Norma had given birth to a cub. Other keepers gathered in the office, and they all discussed how healthy the cub looked. But as Chris watched Norma lick her baby he thought, *This is great, but it's too bad there's only one.* He then noticed that Norma still looked pregnant. Holding his breath, he didn't say anything, and sure enough, a couple of hours later Norma went into labor once more and a second cub "popped out," says Chris. "We were thrilled!" The second cub also appeared to be in great shape, and Norma, who was a new mother, seemed to know exactly how to care for her newborn twins. She nuzzled the cubs and carefully licked them clean.

As with Ivy and her youngster, Norma and her cubs were left alone for about a week—although they were carefully monitored. "It allowed time for them to establish bonds, and as Norma was a very attentive and patient mother," Chris adds, "you could see that she was centered on her cubs." Once Norma and her babies seemed ready for a brief separation, a door connecting the birthing area and another cage was opened, and as Norma entered the other chamber the door was closed. Keepers and zoo veterinarians then safely entered the cage with the cubs and gave them their first health check. They were fine and weighed about two pounds each. Once zoo staffers knew the cubs

were in good shape, they opened the door between the two holding cages so that Norma could have more room to move around. Deciding to take her babies to the adjoining cage, **she picked up the male by the loose skin on the scruff of his neck** and carried him into the new space. "Just like a house cat," says Chris. He wanted to see what Norma would do next. "She had seemed to favor Sasha," remembers Chris. "So, we wondered if she would go back for the female." But patient, caring Norma did exactly that. She definitely seemed to have a very strong sense of family ties.

As time passed, Norma and her cubs were allowed to go into an outside holding area. It was near the exhibit where tigers were on display, but was out of view of visitors so the tigers would not be disturbed. The first time the door opened, the cubs went to the opening, then moved outside, but only a few feet at a time. "They were cautious," says Chris, "but they seemed to like the feel of grass. They would walk for two or three feet, then come back to their mother."

In the outside holding area the cubs explored a whole new world. There were fallen trees to crawl upon and bushes to creep around. They could frolic with each other and their mother, chase her tail, wrestle, and roll around and around like a black-and-orange striped ball. For the cubs it was play, but this was also the schooling that young tigers go through in the wild. By pouncing on Norma, Sasha and Alexis were learning

the same techniques that wild tiger cubs practice—unknowingly—to capture prey. But Norma went a step further. The pigeons, house sparrows, and other wild birds that sometimes land in the Wild Asia exhibit became training objects. Norma taught her cubs to stalk these birds, exactly as she would do in the wild.

**Sasha** and **Alexis** also learned some lessons from Chris and his keepers, and what they taught them would help make life much easier—and safer—for both the cubs and the keepers who cared for them. Make no mistake about it, tigers are dangerous. In the wild they kill other animals in order to eat, and sometimes they kill people—something that also happens occasionally in zoos. It's rare, but every once in a while tigers kill their keepers. It is usually the result of a mistake, by either the tiger or the keeper, and zoo visitors often forget that some of the large creatures they are watching, such as tigers, lions, and even elephants, are wild animals. When flustered, they may react like the wild animals they are, and if a keeper is not on his or her toes, the results can be tragic.

Even so, keepers must work very closely with tigers, as the cats must go inside at night and sometimes be moved from one enclosure to another. Keepers cannot just go into an enclosure and guide a tiger around, so how do they do it? First, keepers help the tigers get used to them. By conditioning, the cats learn, for example, that if they go inside at a certain time, they will be fed. After Sasha and Alexis were born, Chris and his keepers wanted to establish really strong ties with the cubs, so on a regular basis they separated Norma from the cubs, then went into the enclosure with them. The keepers would simply sit there, quietly, allowing the cubs to become accustomed to them. At first the cubs were unsure and kept their distance, but gradually they came to accept the keepers' presence. One day as Chris sat with the cubs Sasha began to approach him. The cub took a few steps, stopped, then took a few more steps. "Come on, boy," Chris said to himself. "Come on." When Sasha was within a foot or so of Chris, he slowly put out his hand and held his breath. Suddenly a wet nose was touching his hand, as Sasha sniffed him. Then, the cub scurried back to Alexis, but Chris was overjoyed. Soon the cubs were happy to see Chris and his keepers enter the enclosure. They **purred and chuffled, which is a sound that tigers make when they are feeling friendly**. If you blow air through your slightly opened lips, you can chuffle too.

Next, Chris and his people decided to train the cubs in a way never tried before with tigers at the zoo. "We thought it would be very helpful if, as adults, they would respond to certain signals," says Chris. "We taught them to roll over, to open their mouths, and to stand with their forepaws on the wire." These behaviors were not circus tricks—they were to help keepers

check over the condition of the cubs once they were too large to handle. The cubs quickly learned to respond to hand signals and the sound of a whistle. It was no wonder, though, since whenever they did as they were told, they received a reward—a juicy meatball. When the cubs were three months old, they were put in the outside exhibit along with their mother. Visitors riding past Wild Asia on the zoo monorail were delighted to see **a happy tiger family, live in the flesh.** But if you think the cubs are fond of Chris, you should hear how attached he's become to them. Reflecting back on the first time Sasha sniffed his hand, he says, "It was totally rewarding. It hit me deep in my soul. It's moments like these that are one of the most wonderful benefits of my job." ■

# CHAPTER 4

# A SAFE HAVEN

Deep in the jungles of Borneo, a huge island that lies off the coast of Southeast Asia, a great snake prowls the forest floor. She is a reticulated python, and her ancient ancestors, which looked very much like her, slid through green jungles at the end of the dinosaur age. *Reticulated* is a word that means "having markings like a net," and the skin of a reticulated python is indeed marked with bronzy patches, outlined in black, that resemble netting. This pattern helps the snake blend into the shadows, leaves, and other foliage on the jungle floor, where it lives and hunts.

The python travels slowly forward by flexing two sets of powerful muscles. One set raises scales on her belly, in ripple fashion from head to tail, and as these scales grip the ground another set of muscles pulls the python ahead. She moves silently, except for an occasional rustle of brush or leaves. She is a very large snake, and it is her size that eventually saves her life and leads her to her new home at the Bronx Zoo. There she will be known as Samantha, one of **the many animals that the zoo has rescued** from an uncertain, even deadly, future. And while Samantha may not know it, the zoo has become not only her home, but also her own personal safe haven.

## Samantha's Tale

A week or so before, back in the Bornean jungle, **Samantha** had finally digested her last dinner of a mouse deer, but she was still hungry. A mouse deer stands a foot high at the shoulder and weighs about ten pounds. But this is only a snack for a large python, which sometimes swallows animals, such as wild pigs, weighing in the neighborhood of one hundred pounds,

and Samantha needed something more to eat. But Samantha was not the only hunter in the steaming tropical forest. Others, on two legs, were also on the prowl. They were leather traders, hunting snakes for their skins. The same reticulated pattern that camouflaged Samantha and helped her survive also put her in great danger at the hands of humans. Her glossy skin could be converted into beautiful and expensive boots, belts, handbags, and other leather accessories.

The traders, about a half dozen of them, were fanned out on the forest floor. Experienced jungle hands, they scanned the branches of the smaller trees scattered among the jungle giants. They knew that some snakes, including pythons, often ascend trees in search of prey, but they also surveyed the ground, which was shaded by the green roof of leaves above. When a movement on the forest floor caught the eye of one trader, he turned to look and gasped. The python at his feet was bigger than any snake he had ever seen before.

"There!" he whispered to his companions, but when they saw the python, their eyes widened. Here was a prize, indeed. Moving slowly, they encircled the python, preparing for a rush. Samantha, sensing that something was not right, turned her head from side to side, flicking her tongue out to sense their position, but it was too late. "Pin it down," one yelled. "But watch out for its teeth," hollered another. This was quite a warning—pythons are not venomous, but they have large, curved teeth that can deliver a horrendous bite. The traders took out nooses and snake sticks, designed to pin a snake to the ground, and although Samantha thrashed and hissed, it was no use. She was a captive and her doom was certainly sealed.

## PRETTY BIG PYTHONS

More than a dozen species of pythons inhabit Africa, Asia, and Australia, and many of them grow to great lengths. The reticulated python, in particular, can measure more than twenty-five feet; the African rock python grows to more than twenty feet, and the Indian python is almost as long. Smaller pythons include the five-foot ball python of Africa and the eight-foot black-headed python of Australia.

Pythons feed mostly on mammals and birds, but the larger pythons can swallow creatures as large as pigs and small deer. A python attacks by grabbing the victim in its jaws, then it wraps its coils around its prey and tightens. Eventually the prey stops breathing and is swallowed by the snake. ◆

It was December 18, 1991, and winter was approaching. The leaves on the oaks, maples, and tulip trees that make the Bronx Zoo a wooded oasis in the city had fallen. A chilly, late-autumn wind rattled the branches, and wild ducks splashed down in the zoo's waterfowl ponds. Some were heading south, and for them the ponds were a welcome stopover, while others were zoo ducks that were mingling with the visitors from far away. In the zoo's reptile and amphibians building, which is known as the World of Reptiles, supervisor Bill Holmstrom was looking at a letter. He and the keepers who work under him feed the animals, clean their enclosures, and watch over their general well-being. Bill and his keepers also assist the scientific staff in their efforts **to breed reptiles and amphibians in captivity**. As Bill began to read the letter he realized it

had come from a leather company in Wisconsin. The letter explained that the company's representatives in Borneo had captured a huge python, which was being housed in an abandoned railroad boxcar. They claimed that the python they had captured was immense, and photographs of the snake were enclosed with the letter. Since the early 1900s the Wildlife Conservation Society had had a standing reward that is now $50,000 for anyone who could deliver a live, healthy snake thirty or more feet in length, so the leather company was sure that their python was a candidate for the prize.

Over the years a handful of people had tried to claim the reward; however, none of their snakes quite measured up. It is very easy to overestimate the length of a large snake, but it is also very difficult to measure one. A snake, more than fifteen feet in length is so strong that **even a dozen strong men cannot straighten it out without kinks**. Its body is continually contracting and squirming, and the more its holders struggle, the harder the snake fights, making the measuring job tougher. So, needless to say, most measurements are at least slightly

off the mark. The interesting fact, however, was that the snake described in the letter was a reticulated python, and this was very intriguing to Bill and his boss, John Behler, the curator of the Reptile Department.

The reticulated python is one of the top two candidates for the title of the world's largest snake. The other is the anaconda of South America, and like the python, the anaconda kills its prey by constriction. For centuries there have been reports filtering out of jungles about reticulated pythons and anacondas that are well over thirty feet long, but none have been fully accepted by scientists. This is not to say that these snakes never exceed thirty feet, as many scientists believe they may. In fact, a python supposedly thirty-two feet long was killed many years ago on the island of Sulawesi, not far from Borneo, and engineers probing the jungles of South America once reported that they had shot an anaconda that was thirty-seven feet long. But regardless of the stories, a live snake more than thirty feet long has never been provided.

John, Bill, and other Wildlife Conservation Society staff members discussed the leather company's offer and decided that even if the snake didn't measure up, bringing it to the Bronx Zoo would surely rescue it from an unpleasant end. Reticulated pythons are becoming scarce in the wild, as the killing for their skins has reduced their numbers. They are also dwindling because the forests in which they live are being destroyed, mainly from lumbering and clearing for development.

"Let's give it a try," said John of the company's offer, but it took more than a year to complete the deal with the

### A GRANDE ANACONDA

Anacondas and pythons are related, but there are some major differences. Both, of course, constrict their prey, but whereas pythons lay eggs that hatch into young snakes, anacondas bear live young that are mini replicas of their mother and father. Anacondas also live mostly in and around water, but pythons, although they can swim, spend most of their time on land. In addition, an anaconda is generally much heavier than a python of the same length. A nineteen-foot anaconda that lived in the Bronx Zoo many years ago weighed 236 pounds, while Samantha, the reticulated python, weighed 250 pounds at twenty-four feet long. If there were a contest for the longest snake in the world, scientists say it would definitely be either the reticulated python or the anaconda. The biggest? Probably the anaconda, but one can never be sure, because measuring snakes—anacondas or otherwise—is sure a slippery business. ♦

leather company. Letters and telephone calls went back and forth for months, and then finally arrangements had to be made for transporting the snake in a sound, healthy condition. International agreements require legal documents for shipping wild animals between countries, so lots of paperwork was involved. Even so, the negotiations took longer than usual. There are suspicions that the leather company was stalling in hopes that the python would grow even larger while it lived in the boxcar and they would win the big Bronx Zoo reward. But finally, after waiting and waiting, it was a go. John was all set to travel to Borneo to bring the snake back to the safety of the zoo, but then he realized something: It was Ramadan. Ramadan is the ninth month of the Islamic year and is also a holy time of fasting and penance when many routine activities slow to a halt. Since most people of Borneo are Islamic, the python shipment was going to have to wait.

When Ramadan was over, Samantha was ready to be shipped to her new home at the Bronx Zoo, but John Behler would not be the one who would take her there. He was bound for the island of Madagascar, off the southeastern coast of Africa, where he is an expert on the local animal and plant life. A replacement escort for

Samantha had to be found. Luckily, the zoo dispatched a reptile importer from Colorado to pick up the python, and Samantha's trip to New York City went without a hitch. Bill Holmstrom and five of his keepers were there to meet her, and so was Dr. William G. Conway, then president of the Wildlife Conservation Society and director of the Bronx Zoo.

Samantha had been shipped in a large burlap sack inside a wooden crate. But along the way the burlap had rotted, and when the crate was opened, Bill and his keepers found themselves looking at one big python, roaming free in the crate. Moving quickly, they placed a tarpaulin over it, one of the keepers grabbed the python behind the head, and everyone else held on to its body. "She was all we could handle," Bill remembers.

Samantha had become accustomed to captivity and to being handled by people, and although she tried to twist and coil her body, she did not put up a difficult struggle. The keepers stretched her out on the floor as best they could, and Bill and Dr. Conway got onto their hands and knees to measure her. No doubt about it, she was a giant—but as they had thought, she was not the prizewinner. The length of the tape, which was actually just a long cord, indicated that she was only slightly more than twenty-one feet. She also weighed only 150 pounds, which is at least fifty pounds less than expected for a snake of her length. She seemed in good shape, however, so the keepers weren't worried.

"We were a bit disappointed that she wasn't as long as reported," says Bill, but even so, she was longer than any python known to be in an American zoo. Back at the reptile house an enclosure had been prepared for Samantha that contained strong tree limbs and rocks she could climb, and visitors would be able to view her through thick glass covering the front of the enclosure.

After Samantha arrived at the zoo and was checked out by the staff veterinarians, they pronounced her a little too skinny but perfectly fit. Once the reptile staff began feeding her, however, she put on weight and today weighs more than 250 pounds. She has also grown longer and at last count was more than twenty-five feet long. Perhaps if she keeps growing, the Wildlife Conservation Society will win its own reward! Either way, both zoo and snake are perfectly happy with the way things have turned out.

## Three Strikes and You're Out

Huge, powerful, and aggressive, the **grizzly bear** is a creature of the deep wilderness. Once it roamed through western North America from the Pacific Ocean to the prairies, but as the West was settled grizzlies were exterminated from much of their natural range.

Grizzlies can be extremely dangerous to both people and livestock, and an adult grizzly, which can weigh more than six hundred pounds, is strong enough to kill a bison. Grizzlies have also killed and sometimes eaten people, so they are not necessarily the best neighbors.

Grizzlies are still abundant, however, in much of western Canada and Alaska, as well as below the Canadian border, where they inhabit a few areas in wilderness portions of Montana, Idaho, and Wyoming. But even there grizzlies sometimes come into conflict with people. They may encounter hikers and campers in national forests or parks, and occasionally they come out of the wilderness and attack livestock. The federal government protects grizzlies, except when these big bears repeatedly threaten people and their animals. Federal authorities have a rule for grizzlies that are repeat offenders: Three strikes and you're out. If a grizzly kills sheep or cattle, or raids a campsite, it is captured and removed back to the wilderness. The third time it becomes a problem, it will be destroyed unless a home can be found for it.

**The Big Bears exhibit** at the Bronx Zoo is the home of four grizzlies that struck out. They were on the Feds' hit list, but the zoo offered them a home. Their names are **Archie**, **Jughead**, **Betty**, and **Veronica**, named after the characters in the popular comic books, and they are now thriving at their sanctuary in the zoo.

Each one of them got in trouble as a young cub. Archie and Jughead, who are brothers, were born in 1993 in Glacier National Park, Montana. Betty and Veronica came into the world a year earlier, and Betty, like Archie and Jughead, was a Glacier bear, and Veronica came from the Yellowstone National Park region. All four bears seemed to have been driven out of the wilderness areas by larger, older bears. Grizzlies require lots of space in which to live and hunt for food, and with the shrinking wilderness, bigger, tougher bears often chase younger ones out of the best living areas. Frequently, that is when the young bears butt heads with people.

Marty Zyburu is a senior keeper in the Bronx Zoo's Mammal Department, stationed in the Big Bears exhibit. He knows the feeding and care of bears because he has worked with them for years, so when Archie, Jughead, and Betty were captured at Glacier in July 1995, the zoo sent him there to bring them to their new home. But how do you bring three grizzly bears from Montana to New York City in the heat of summer? The zoo called a company that ships cattle, and they sent a trailer truck with two air conditioners mounted on top to meet Marty in Montana. The bears, inside heavy crates of wood with metal bars, were loaded inside, then Marty jumped into the truck's cab alongside the driver, and off they went, back to the Bronx.

For five days Marty and the bears kept on trucking. They started out with a three-day supply of bear food that Marty had brought from the zoo, and after it ran out, Marty stopped at supermarkets and bought sacks of dog food along with lots of fruit and vegetables. Bears, like people, have a varied diet of animal and plant matter. Marty fed the bears in the morning and evening through chutes in their cages. "We would usually pull off the road in a quiet place so we wouldn't attract a crowd," he says. "And we would water them when we stopped for gas, two or three times a day." At night they stopped at motels, parking the trailer outside. "We used small motels so we could keep an eye on the trailer," says Marty.

Occasionally people would suspect that the trailer was carrying unusual cargo. "What's in there?" a man once asked at a gas station when Marty was watering his group. "Bears," replied Marty. "We got a lot of raised eyebrows, but people were quite nice about it," he says, laughing. Plans originally called for the Bronx Zoo to take Archie and Jughead, and for a Midwestern zoo to house Betty. Marty went ahead and dropped her off there, but as things turned out, she would eventually join her buddies in the Bronx.

When the truck reached the Bronx Zoo, it headed for the Wildlife Health Sciences Center, which is a state-of-the-art animal hospital and wellness facility. A forklift brought the crates to the door of the center's quarantine area, where the bears would be staying. All animals arriving at the zoo are kept alone for thirty days or more before they are released into their habitats to make sure that they are not carrying any diseases. It was during this time that Veronica became a problem in the Yellowstone area. She was eventually captured, and the Bronx Zoo agreed to take her as well. Keeper Lee Rosalinski was dispatched to Yellowstone, where Veronica was loaded aboard the same truck that had carried Archie, Jughead, and Betty. As Lee headed east he stopped at the zoo where Betty was living, as it had been decided that she would be happier with the rest of the gang. She was loaded in with Veronica, and the truck took off for the Bronx once again.

After arriving at the zoo, Betty and Veronica were also placed in quarantine, and after all four bears were pronounced healthy, **they were placed in their exhibit**. Archie and Jughead got along famously with Betty and Veronica, but often the boys hang out just with the boys, and the girls with the girls. They have all grown into healthy, happy adult bears, and although they can no longer roam the wild, they are safe, with people who really appreciate them and know how to keep them in the best of shape. They are also doing a favor for their fellow grizzlies in the wild. One of the reasons that zoos exhibit animals is to remind people how wonderful wild creatures are. Signs at the Big Bears exhibit nudge visitors to remember that grizzlies

are animals of the wilderness, and if the wilderness disappears, so will the grizzly.

## Choo Choo

When the parents and grandparents of kids today talk about railroad trains, they often call them "choo-choo" trains. That is because that's the sound steam engines once made when they huffed and puffed along the train tracks, hauling long lines of passenger and freight cars. At the Bronx Zoo there is an owl named Choo Choo. She is an elegant owl, a favorite of visitors and the zoo's Bird Department. She sits on her perch and stares at passersby with big yellow eyes. When a mouse scurries into her enclosure, or a young house sparrow flies in, Choo Choo swoops down from her perch and is on it like a flash. As she grabs the prey with her long talons it is dead meat—literally. Owls are super predators, so it should not be surprising that Choo Choo can catch small rodents and birds. But her ability to do so is remarkable—because Choo Choo cannot fly.

**Choo Choo is a snowy owl.** White with small black markings, she hatched in a nest on the treeless tundra of northern Canada. There, like other snowy owls, she fed largely on lemmings, which are little rodents, and snowshoe hares. Normally, snowy owls remain on the tundra year-round; however, every five to seven years, large numbers of owls leave the tundra during the winter. This occurs when the lemming and snowshoe hare populations dwindle and the owls have to leave in search of food. It was during this time in 1990 when Choo Choo left her perch. "We received many reports of snowy owl sightings that fall," says Chris Sheppard, a curator in the Bird Department. So she was not surprised when, on a Sunday in November, a man called to say that he had seen a snowy owl along a railroad track in the northern Bronx. What was unusual was that the caller, who worked for the railroad, said the owl had been there for several days. "I think she may be hurt," the man told Chris.

Chris sent two keepers to the place where the owl had been seen, and it was indeed injured. Apparently a train had struck the bird, and both of her wings were badly damaged. The keepers rushed the owl to the animal hospital at the zoo, and in order to save her life, the veterinarians made a drastic decision—they had to amputate all of one wing and half of the other. Eventually, Choo Choo was nursed back to health. "We really became attached to her," says Chris. "But she wasn't that friendly. She would snap and hiss at us. But she had dignity and we really wanted to have her at the zoo."

The federal government protects owls like Choo Choo, so in order to keep her, the zoo needed permission from the United States Fish and Wildlife Service. Once it was given, Choo Choo was placed on exhibit, where she remains a favorite of both the staff and the zoo visitors. "But she still hisses at us," says Chris. ■

# CHAPTER 5
# SNAKE BUSTERS

*Late morning, October 9, 1984. Forty-sixth Precinct, New York City Police Department, the South Bronx:*

With an urgent look on his face, a police officer grabs a telephone and quickly dials a number. His fingers drum on the desktop while he waits for an answer, and once he gets it, he identifies himself, then says, "We need help—fast." The officer explains that a potentially dangerous fugitive is holed up in a vacant building on 176th Street in the Bronx. But was the officer calling a special police unit? No way—he was calling the Reptile Department at the Bronx Zoo. That's because the police weren't after a real-life criminal, like we see on TV. They were after a snake. The fugitive in question was a very large snake in a very bad mood, measuring more than thirteen feet long, and the New York City Police Department knew that they needed the help of experts to capture the creature.

"Can you send some people to give us a hand?" the officer asked. "No problem," was the answer, "**we've had plenty of practice handling snakes**. We do it every day."

Almost from the time the Bronx Zoo opened in 1899, the staffers of its Reptile Department have been helping police and other agencies in the New York City area round up snakes on the run. Most of these snakes are not native New Yorkers. The snakes that live in the wild in and around New York City are harmless and often small. They usually stay out of sight and are seldom seen, but those that prompt calls to the Reptile Department are of a different sort. They are usually native to faraway places, such as Asia and Africa, and some of them are very large. Others are venomous, with bites that could prove fatal to a person who got in their way. Usually these snakes are pets that have escaped or have been released by owners who can no longer care for them, and their long-term chances of survival in the city are very low. This is a danger for them and for us, because while they are alive, they scare and at times endanger people.

The Snake Busters are not called into action very

often—only about a half dozen times a year. The main reason Snake Busters are needed by public authorities is that police and animal control people have little experience with snakes—and are seldom sure if a snake is a dangerous species or not. Although these animal control workers have more expertise when it comes to

corralling creatures such as wayward deer or coyotes, snakes are another matter.

**Snakes on the loose turn up in all sorts of strange places.** Sometimes they creep into the walls of buildings or hide under porches. They may curl up in a pile of rubbish or slip into the sewer system. It's hard to believe, but people have even found escaped snakes curled up in their bathroom toilet bowl. Not a good way to start the day.

## The Birth of the Snake Busters

The snake that caused such a problem for the Forty-sixth Precinct had apparently been set loose by a tenant who had to leave his apartment building because of renovations. The snake was a **reticulated python,** native to Southeast Asia, and although pythons are not venomous, they suffocate their prey by constriction and can be particularly dangerous. They are immensely powerful and can bite viciously. In fact, in 1997 a Bronx teenager was accidentally killed after he draped his pet python around his neck and the snake started squeezing.

So when the police got the okay from the Reptile Department, they dispatched a cruiser to pick up a three-person team of zoo staffers to collect the snake. Supervisor Peter Brazaitis and then-keepers Bill Holmstrom and Kathy Gerety gathered their snake tongs and hooks, a covered barrel, a canvas bag, and leather gloves, and when the cruiser arrived, they were waiting.

Sirens blasting and lights blazing, the cruiser sped the team through the South Bronx to the abandoned building. The building where the python had been found was being renovated, and standing four stories high, it was a skeleton of its old self. Its halls were filled with rubbish, and workers were tearing down its interior walls and boarding up its windows. As part of the renovation process an electrician was stripping old electrical cables out of the walls, getting the shock of his life when he pulled on one cable and it yanked back. "It took me off my feet," he later told police, still shaken from the experience.

When not looking for a meal or a mate, snakes like to hide. That's what this python did, except he left his tail dangling from a hole in the wall. Working fast, the electrician was snatching as many cables as he could from the wall, when he realized that this cable was alive, but not with electricity.

The cruiser carrying the Bronx Zoo team screeched to a halt outside the building, where the scene resembled that of a hostage situation. Police cruisers had sealed off the area with barricades, and many neighborhood residents, curious about what was happening, had gathered around the building. A police van was parked in front, its motor running, and officers had already gone inside the structure. The zoo team scrambled up a temporary wooden staircase to the third floor, where they found that the cops had managed to snag the

snake with a capture pole—a hollow metal rod with a noose at the end—normally used to catch stray dogs. The police had the snake in custody, but they did not know what do with it. Read it its rights? Not likely. The python was understandably cranky as it **thrashed about, hissing and showing its wicked teeth.**

"What the devil do we do now?" an officer asked the zoo team. Without so much as a word, the Snake Busters set to work. One grabbed the snake behind the head, while another took hold of the middle of its body and a third clamped down on its tail. "Ease off on the noose," Peter told the police, and as the noose was removed the zoo team bundled the snake into the bag, placed it in the barrel, and clamped the lid tightly shut. Escorted by police, the zoo's snake catchers hauled the barrel toward the cruiser, as the onlooking crowd pressed forward, eager to see the snake. Moving quickly, the police bundled the zoo team and the snake into the cruiser, and off they went, back to the zoo.

The snake was placed in the zoo's reptile building, and upon examination it was found to be very thin for a python of its size. It weighed only forty pounds, which is less than half of what it should have weighed. The python was eventually nursed back to health, becoming sleek and fat, but at that time the Bronx Zoo did not need another reticulated python in its collection, so the snake that had caused all the fuss ended up going to live in a zoo in New Jersey.

After the zoo team brought the python back to the

reptile building, however, they gathered together and discussed the day's events. Kathy Gerety, a member of the rescue team, went to the blackboard and, taking a cue from an emblem used in the film *Ghostbusters*, drew **a coiled python with a circle around it**, slashed by a diagonal line. With the addition of the name Snake Busters, it became the official logo for the zoo's Reptile

Department. Later, Peter Brazaitis embellished the symbol with the words *Valor, Humility, Greed, Fear, Senility, Pain.*

"Those are the attributes of a reptile keeper," he says. And everyone at the zoo knows not to mess with the Snake Busters.

## Sssss-urprises

Pythons figure into a large number of Snake Busters cases, as many people who keep snakes as pets are impressed by the python's large size. The problem is, once it grows to that size, they are pretty difficult to handle, and some python owners, like the one in the Bronx, take the easy way out by letting their pet go without caring what happens to it or to the other animals and people it might encounter.

On August 1, 1993, the Snake Busters received a call from the city of Mt. Vernon, New York. People reported seeing a three-foot boa constrictor lurking around their neighborhood. Keeper Peter Taylor and Steve Rodriguez, a Snake Busters volunteer who had experience with handling reptiles, responded. A surprise awaited them, however, because the snake was not a boa. It was a python and was much bigger than they were expecting.

When they arrived at the house, the Snake Busters found a crowd gathered, and several adults were shouting suggestions on how to track down the snake. "We saw it go under the porch," said one. "We threw rocks at it and hit it with a stick, but then we couldn't see it anymore. It's down there someplace." A group of boys had also gathered, ready to spring into action and armed to the teeth with water pistols, a BB gun, and sticks. One even held a can of fuel oil in case they had to smoke the snake out.

The two Snake Busters crawled into the darkness under the porch and moved very carefully. The "boa" could just as easily turn out to be a venomous snake, and meeting it under cramped conditions might be a no-win situation. With his flashlight Taylor probed the darkness only to see an obstacle course of junk that had been tossed under the porch over the last few years. After almost an hour in the dark the Snake Busters, sweating in the ninety-degree heat, came up empty. As a last resort, however, they went back down to scout out the foundation of the porch, where there was a pile of old tires. Taylor and his partner had begun removing the tires, one by one, when they struck pay dirt. Curled up among rubbish and some old pieces of shelving was a reticulated python measuring about ten feet long.

The Snake Busters risked a dangerous bite if they simply reached in and grabbed the python, so instead they poked the snake with a stick. It moved just enough for Steve to grab its tail, and for Peter to grab its middle. As they pulled at the snake they realized it was no use. The python had braced itself against the shelving and gained leverage. The powerful muscles that enable pythons to constrict their prey were now pulling the snake toward a hole in the foundation.

Frantically Peter tossed more rubbish aside to expose the snake, while Steve hauled at the python's tail. One moment the snake would lose ground, then the next moment it would inch ahead. Finally, after what seemed forever, the Snake Busters pulled the snake from its hiding place with one powerful heave. Dirty and tired, the Snake Busters emerged from beneath the porch, and their watchers cheered. The python was in relatively good shape, although it was rather skinny, weighing only eighteen pounds. Back at the zoo the python, which turned out to be a female, was given all the food she needed. She proved to be quite a chowhound, however, even for a python, and after nine months of feeding had eaten eighty-eight rats and two rabbits. It's a good thing she was caught, because she was one hungry snake!

**Forbidden Fruit?**

Many years ago Reptile Department staffers were frequently asked to catch snakes that had stowed away in shipments of fruit, especially bananas. Today, refrigeration and thorough examination of shipments have cut down on the number of stowaways, but it still sometimes happens. A few years ago the Snake Busters handled just such a case. Bill Holmstrom, supervisor of the reptile collection, received a call from a sergeant in the New York City Police. He told Bill that a **rattlesnake** was loose in a refrigerated trailer full of honeydew melons at Hunts Point Market, a produce distribution center in the Bronx. Workers had locked the rear doors of the trailer, but nobody was about to enter it.

Bill advised the police to lower the temperature in the trailer, as snakes grow inactive when the temperature cools, then Bill and keeper Rich Zerilli got into a car and headed for Hunts Point, a ten-minute drive from the zoo. The sergeant had given them directions, but he obviously did not know the way, because the Snake Busters became hopelessly lost for an hour.

Eventually they blundered into Hunts Point and found more than a dozen workers and several cops lined up on a warehouse loading dock, all of them staring at the locked doors of the trailer. The rattler had been spotted by a forklift operator who was unloading wooden crates of melons. When the **rattler started buzzing,** the operator panicked, dropped his load and jumped off the machine. The forklift tilted on its side, and the crates crashed down and melons bounced all over the inside of the trailer. With broken boxes and heaps of melons everywhere, the snake had plenty of places to hide. Slowly the Snake Busters opened the doors. The interior of the truck was like a damp, frosty cave, with broken boxes and melons on the floor, and more crates stacked on wooden pallets at the back. The first task was to clear off the floor of the truck, so the Snake Busters asked the workers to help. "Not on your life," one replied. "There's a rattlesnake in there."

It took the Snake Busters ten minutes to clear off the

floor, but they didn't find the snake, so they began to check out the stacked crates. Under the first row was the rattler—it was small, less than a yard long, and just like they thought, the cool temperature had made it inactive. The Snake Busters picked it up with a pair of snake tongs and placed it in a barrel. Once the serpent was removed, the workers entered the truck. The snake they had found was identified as a southern Pacific rattlesnake, and it had traveled with the melons from California. For a year it lived at the Bronx Zoo, then it embarked on another long journey: It was transferred all the way to a zoo in Europe that wanted to exhibit a southern Pacific rattlesnake. So the melon rattler that liked to hitchhike got another free ride. ■

## CHAPTER 6

# JUST LIKE HOME

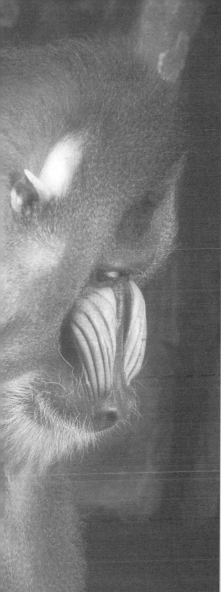

**"I** guess it's time to put them in," said Jerry Johnson as he was finishing lunch one day in the early 1960s with Bronx Zoo curator Lee Crandall. "Them" referred to a family of mandrills that were ready for their new home. **Mandrills** are really just big baboons, and a male mandrill can weigh more than a hundred pounds. But since baboons are actually monkeys, mandrills are considered the world's largest living monkeys. They are also the most bizarre-looking monkeys, as the male mandrill sports some of the brightest colors of any mammal. Its cheeks are purple and blue, and separating the cheeks is a nose and muzzle that is dazzling scarlet. Mandrills live only in the deepest West African forests, and because they live in the remote wilderness, they are not easy for scientists to observe.

Jerry Johnson, who was curator of the zoo's Design Department, and Lee Crandall, whose specialty was with mammals, headed to the zoo's Monkey House, where members of the Mammal Department were waiting. They were all standing around a brand-new exhibit that was still empty. It had been designed to look just like a slice of West African forest, but though it looked real, it wasn't. Everything from the huge forest tree in the middle of the exhibit down to the cascade of vines and branches was really made of fiberglass.

As this was one of the first exhibits of its kind, the zoo wasn't sure how the animals would react. At the time the exhibit in the Monkey House was opened, little was known about mandrills, and most of it came from watching them in zoos. Even today scientists have not unraveled all the mysteries of how they live, so when the family, headed by a huge male, was released

# THE BIRTH OF THE NEW ZOO

The Bronx Zoo has led the way when it comes to developing modern zoo exhibits that simulate wild habitats. In 1964 it opened the first major zoo building completely devoted to this type of exhibit. Called the Aquatic Birds Building, it continues to be one of the most popular exhibits in the zoo, and over the years zoo visitors have seen the world of waterbirds at close range. They have watched boat-billed herons nesting in treetops that are at eye level because they are planted in sunken cages. Visitors have also seen little shorebirds scampering across sand beaches washed by waves created with machinery.

Ironically, this building is the oldest one at the zoo and has been there since the zoo's opening-day ceremony in 1899. From the beginning it was a building for birds; however, as years passed the building aged, and it was no longer used to exhibit animals. Its only purpose was as a winter home for aquatic birds that had to be removed from outdoor exhibits when the cold weather descended. The zoo's director, Dr. William G. Conway, had long wished to create exhibits that would truly teach people how animals behave naturally in the wild, as well as exhibits that would make animals feel comfortable and encourage them to breed. Exhibit designer Jerry Johnson was new to the zoo, so Conway assigned him the task of converting the aging building into the most advanced zoo exhibit anywhere. It wasn't long before work also began on the **Monkey House exhibit** that would forever change the way zoos were viewed.   ◆

into the exhibit, everyone held their breath. The mandrills looked around, then touching the branches and vines, they began to explore. As if they had wandered into an unfamiliar area of a real forest, the mandrills began to acquaint themselves with their new home. But it wasn't a new experience just for the monkeys—it was unfamiliar territory for the zoo staffers, too. This was an early example of how zoos create exhibits that mimic the natural habitat of the animals housed in them.

At first the male sat for a moment by the huge roots of the tree, then he scrambled up them and, to the delight of watchers, rubbed his chest against the trunk. There was an important reason behind his behavior. He was rubbing his scent from glands on his chest against the trunk, marking it his territory. This action had been reported only a few times by scientists, and even Mr. Crandall, an expert on mammals, remarked, "I've heard of it, but never have seen it before." The mandrill exhibit was so natural that the male behaved just as his species normally does in the wild. It was a wonderful accomplishment for the zoo, and was just the beginning, as zoos all over the country started changing their exhibits over from stark metal cages to lush, foliage-covered exhibits. Working with staffers from animal departments, zoo designers now build exhibits that make not only animals, but people, feel as though they are actually in some of the world's wildest places.

### Congo Gorilla Forest

Mandrills still live at the zoo, but their home today is even more natural and exciting than the Monkey House exhibit was years ago. Now they live in a **human-made jungle** that most experts view as the most advanced and impressive zoo exhibit in the world. It is the Congo Gorilla Forest.

It's fall 1998, and sounds of construction

# PROFILE: JOHN GWYNNE

John Gwynne heads the best-known design department of any zoo in the world. For him, it's a dream job. He pursues his interests in artistic fields and in animals as well. Like most zoo people, he developed a curiosity about animals at an early age. He grew up in a small town in rural Rhode Island, where he "spent time poking around ponds looking for tadpoles and frogs," he says. He was also fascinated with art, so at college he majored in biology and art history. While he was there, a friend of his began writing a field guide to birds. When he was finished, he asked John to illustrate it. "I had never painted birds before," says John, "but I accepted." By the time John was finished, he had illustrated more than a thousand birds.

But right before John graduated, a professor suggested that he become a landscape architect. So John went on to graduate school, where he decided to combine his knowledge of design, architecture, and biology. After graduating in 1974, he went home to Rhode Island and read in the newspaper that the small Roger Williams Park Zoo was undergoing renovation. Located in Providence, the zoo was in horrible disrepair, so John contacted the zoo director and asked if they needed a designer. Since the zoo had no funds of its own to hire one, the director replied that there were only government funds available at the time to hire someone. "The pay was terrible," says John. "But it was an opportunity, and I took it." John went on to head the zoo's exhibits and graphics operation. "My office was in an old stable with a skunk living in it," says John. But John jumped headfirst into his work and helped revitalize the zoo, which today is considered one of the better zoos in the United States. In fact, some of the exhibits he designed won awards, and as his reputation grew he eventually found a home at the world-renowned Bronx Zoo.  ♦

come from a site in one corner of the Bronx Zoo, where carpenters, plumbers, electricians, horticulturists, and design technicians are hard at work. They are building a forest, and John Gwynne, the zoo's director for design, is on site, talking to a visitor. "It's coming along well," he says, "but we can't let up. This exhibit has to be opened next year, which is only a few months away."

John is speaking about the Congo Gorilla Forest, which is probably the most ambitious zoo exhibit ever attempted. It is so revolutionary that zoo officials suspect that it will take a year or two after opening to work out any possible kinks. That's no matter, as the **Congo Gorilla Forest is truly an exhibit for the twenty-first century.** Animals have never lived in such

an exhibit before, nor have people ever walked through one like it. It is designed to make both people and animals feel as though they are in a real African rain forest—not an easy task to accomplish.

The Congo Gorilla Forest itself covers six and a half acres, which is larger than some small zoos, and although most of it is outside, it also includes a core building of 37,000 square feet. The forest is home to two families of lowland gorillas, one headed by the famous Timmy. The forest is also occupied by okapis; **mandrills; red river hogs,** which are wild pigs; monkeys called guenons; hornbills; pygmy geese; pythons; electric fish; and all sorts of invertebrates, such as millipedes.

This remarkable zoo exhibit is a patchwork of shady forest, treetop lookouts, rock cliffs, streams

and pools, bamboo thickets, and open meadows. **Parts of it are natural and others are artificial**, made by the zoo exhibit staff. Many of the trees and shrubs in the forest were there before the exhibit was built, but others have been planted to fill it in even more. Some of the vegetation in the forest consists of cold-weather relatives of plants that actually grow in tropical Africa, which would surely perish during the harsh New York winters. And since most of the animals in the Congo Gorilla Forest live on plants, people often wonder why they don't eat the exhibit bare. This is because zoo designers have outsmarted them, or have at least tried to. Many of the plants that animals might feed on are placed out of reach, but mostly it is a matter of using plants they do not like to eat. For example, Wildlife Conservation Society scientists in Africa noticed that okapis avoided one type of plant, the way some kids avoid broccoli. This plant would have been ideal for the okapi exhibit, but it would not grow in New York, so a cold-weather relative that resembles its tropical cousin was used, making the okapi habitat look more natural. And like its African relative, it was avoided by the zoo okapis too.

## Can a Pig Be Beautiful?

With its gorgeous copper-colored fur and white whiskers, the **red river hog** of the Congo forest is considered one of the most beautiful pigs on the planet. Red river hogs are one of the many animal species living in the zoo's Congo Gorilla Forest. In the wild, red river hogs, which can weigh up to 250 pounds, ramble

through the forest in groups that sometimes number in the hundreds. They have been **called living bulldozers** because they root up everything in their path in search of nuts, roots, and just about anything else they can find to eat. But given their destructive habits, how on earth did the Bronx Zoo create an environmental exhibit for these creatures? Not to mention that they have to live with mandrills and monkeys?

First of all, the mandrills and monkeys don't seem to mind the hogs, and secondly, the mandrills and monkeys spend most of their time on the high forested hillsides and in the treetops of the exhibit. The hogs live down below, where a stream flows. As their name implies, red river hogs like to live along watercourses, and the hillsides are a yard or more above the stream, higher than the hogs want to travel. "Pigs don't fly," jokes John Gwynne.

The big problem with exhibiting red river hogs, however, is keeping them from destroying the exhibit. They cannot destroy the foliage above the stream because they do not climb up to it, but what about the stream area itself? The zoo wants the hogs to behave normally—rooting about—but needs to keep the exhibit in shape as well. Cleverly, the edges of the stream are lined with sandy areas, just as in nature, where the keepers hide vegetables, fruit, and peanuts in the sand each day. But in the morning, before the hogs are let

out of their holding area into the exhibit, keepers rake down the sand and plant the food, so the hogs can start their daily routine once again.

The vegetation in the Congo exhibit is **a combination of both artificial and natural plants**. The artificial vegetation is generally made of fiberglass covered by a plastic resin and then painted to look realistic. Visitors walk among the huge lower trunks of man-made jungle trees, which at first glance, are almost impossible to distinguish from the real thing. Rubber vines are laced between the trees, and live vines have gradually grown up to creep over the artificial ones, creating a tangle that truly resembles the roof of an African forest. This impression is fostered, however, by fine wire netting used to keep animals such as mandrills and monkeys from climbing

out of their exhibits. The netting, hardly visible to the eye, has been covered with live vines, and it adds to the feeling that both visitors and animals are deep in the forest. It is also quite amazing when you realize that a few hundred yards away are the busy city streets of the Bronx. Yet in the exhibit visitors walk among animals that most people would never see except in the wild. This exhibit is truly a work of art. It seems so real that travelers walking through the forest often feel as if stepping off the trail will mean being lost in the wilderness forever.

## THE COOLEST CLASSROOM

The Bronx Zoo built the Congo Gorilla Forest not only to create an environment that would encourage gorillas to breed, but also to directly involve visitors in the conservation of the African forest and the creatures that live there—and have fun doing it. Through hands-on experience visitors can learn how scientists are studying the forest and its animals. At one station in the exhibit, for instance, visitors can track the okapis by radio telemetry, just as scientists do in the forest. Other stations have computers that provide interactive experiences that promote learning, and inside the central building visitors can enter a theater and watch an on-screen presentation about the forest. When the movie is over, up goes the screen, and behind it live gorillas can be seen hanging out and enjoying their day at the zoo. And hidden atop the

exhibit's building is an education center, where the **programs conducted for students are brought alive.** From the center students can observe the gorillas and other animals of the forest, and in a sense the animals become the teachers.                                                               ♦

The path through the forest is about a quarter mile long, but it seems much longer because of all the twists and turns. Visitors walking along the trail often see the same exhibits, but from many different angles. This technique makes visitors feel as if they are seeing new areas of forest all along the way. The path winds through woodlands and past rock faces, and at one point enters a canyon with rock walls that tower twenty-five feet high. The rocks are not real, of course, but are made of a special type of concrete shot from a spray gun over banks of earth by construction crews. Real rocks are scattered among the artificial creations, so even experts must look closely to tell the difference. Naturally, the animals are everywhere, but they are separated from the public and act much as they do in the real forest. Jungle sounds ring through the air, and here and there clouds of mist twist around the trees. Along the way the path loops through an artificial fallen log, but at eighty feet long and ten feet in diameter, it feels more like a tunnel. It is a replica of a fallen tree that has partially rotted, but inside there are hidden cages on the walls where millipedes shine like polished stones. When visitors come upon breaks in the log, they can catch glimpses of okapis moving among the greenery. As the path nears its end it crosses through the most

dramatic part of the Congo Gorilla Forest. Here **visitors walk through a glass tunnel** that separates the forest's two gorilla exhibits, as the gorillas climb and swing all around them.

The animals feel perfectly at home in the exhibit, as it contains everything they need: places where they can feed, relax, romp, and have a bit of privacy. Zoo technicians have also developed devices that promote natural behavior in the animals. For years the Bronx Zoo has been developing a process called enrichment. Before the Congo Gorilla Forest was built, peanut butter was hidden in cracks  within logs in the gorilla exhibit so the gorillas would hunt for it, but things have become much more sophisticated these days. Now, for instance, the Congo exhibit is filled with artificial trees that are actually electronically timed feeders, which encourage gorillas to explore in search of food, as they do in the wild. Some hidden feeders are placed near the front of exhibits, making it easier for people to see the animals, while others—in the mandrill habitat, for instance—are hidden in

## ROCK, PAPER, SCISSORS, AND TREES?

Many of the materials used to recreate natural environments in zoos can be found in your own home or around you. The rubber and plastic used to create rocks and vines in many of the exhibits is the same material that is used to make common items like toothbrushes and plastic dishes. The vines, however, have ropes or chains at their core and are covered with flexible rubbery plastic, almost like bungee cords. And believe it or not, the fiberglass used to make an artificial tree is the same substance used to make boats and cars. The zoo designers have simply adapted these materials to recreate the natural world, with everything from monkeys to millipedes.                 ♦

artificial rocks. Perhaps the most clever feeder of all is in the Great Gorilla Building. It is built to look like a termite mound and provides a view to the public. If a gorilla approaches the mound, visitors standing just a foot or so away can see the gorilla reach into the mound and chow down. It is a beneficial way for the gorillas to hunt for their own food and for the people who come to learn about them.

Many of the techniques used to create the Congo Gorilla Forest are based on observations documented by the Wildlife Conservation Society scientists. One team of scientists, for instance, found that lowland gorillas seek shelter from rain and heat inside hollow trees. So, close by the glass in the central building, designers built a cross section of a rotted tree, with its open side facing the public. Visitors to the forest will also sometimes notice mandrills sitting on rocks, especially on cool days. These rocks are known as "hot rocks," or "baboon bun warmers," as the people at the zoo laughingly call them. Inside the rocks are heating elements, so when it gets chilly, the mandrills head for the rocks and take a seat to warm up.

## Do Good Fences Make Good Neighbors?

The fancy rock warmers are also used in another of the
Bronx Zoo's baboon exhibits—the Ethiopian Baboon
Reserve, home to the gelada baboons. Found only in
the mountains of central Ethiopia, these baboons spend
the night in rocky gorges, and in the morning they
climb up onto grassy plateaus, where they feed on
grasses, roots, and bulbs. In the spring of 1990 the zoo
opened a two-acre exhibit based on this kind of plateau.
But just as they began construction they realized they had
a few challenges.

"We wanted to do what no zoo had ever done before," says Jim Doherty, the zoo's general curator, "and we knew it would involve some fancy thinking." The zoo wanted to exhibit two troops of **gelada baboons** in the same area and weren't sure if they would get along. A gelada troop usually consists of one adult male and about a half dozen females and their young. Although troops sometimes gather together to feed, especially when food is plentiful, mostly the troops demand their own space. Gelada males have huge, sharp canine teeth and have been known to fight viciously. Their battles are usually waged because one is trying to steal away with the other one's females. Ironically, the females fight almost as much, though it is typically nonviolent and involves only a lot of charging, yowling, and slapping of their arms.

Since the females are less aggressive, Jim decided to teach them to get along first. He strung a length of hot wire fence, which is

---

### CONGO GORILLA FOREST FACTS

**Size:** 6.5 acres

**Claim to fame:** world's largest African forest exhibit

**Features:** 30,000 square feet of artificial rock outcrops, more than 20,000 plants of 400 species

**Animals:** More than 400 animals of 55 species, including thirty-three gorillas, the largest breeding group in North America

♦

used with domestic livestock that would deliver a mild electrical shock if touched, diagonally across the exhibit and released the females of one troop on one side of the wire. They stayed away from the barrier and, after a couple of weeks, became accustomed to their space. Then they were taken inside and the other troop's females were released on their own side of the wire. They, too, became used to their piece of territory after a while and were brought back inside. The next step, however, was to put the first troop back out on its side of the wire, with its adult male. Jim knew that the male, although the leader, usually stays calm as long as the females do, so when they were released into the exhibit, Jim was pleased to see they seemed perfectly at home. After a few days the first troop went back in, and the second troop, with its male, came out for a trial period. They, too, were at ease.

Everything seemed to be going according to plan, but the exhibit was due to open soon and it was approaching crunch time. So one morning both groups of females were released, each on its own side of the wire. Jim and his keepers stood by with nets and water-powered fire extinguishers to separate the baboons in case of trouble. The two groups of females ran to the fence. They challenged one another by screaming and jumping up and down, but that was it, and eventually each group quieted down.

"After a few days," says Jim, "we removed the wire fence, and they didn't bother each other anymore. Each group was at home in its own territory."

A few more days passed, and Jim knew it was time to introduce the males. The wire was reinstalled, and both baboon troops, with their males, went into the exhibit. Everyone was tense, ready to intervene at a moment's notice, knowing that a **big baboon can deliver a very big bite.** When the baboons finally came out, everyone held their breath, but the baboons scarcely even looked at one another. Each troop felt totally at home in its own space, and after a few days the zoo removed the wire again. When the baboons went out the next morning, they acted as if the wire were still there, and everybody breathed a sigh of relief. It wasn't long, however, before the two troops switched spaces, and amazingly enough, did so without any quarreling. Maybe the baboons had become bored with their living area, or perhaps, like many people, they just needed a change of scene. One can never know, but after that the two troops began to wander peacefully throughout the exhibit, so much so that a third and fourth troop were eventually added.

It is this sort of understanding of animal behavior, along with patience and willingness to experiment, that makes such a great zoo exhibit. Now the geladas of the Bronx Zoo's exhibit can wander their two-acre grassland in individual troops but share the entire area, much as wild gelada baboons come together to feed in the real Ethiopian highlands.

## Building an Underground City
Often, **designing a very small exhibit can be as tricky, and challenging** as creating one that covers acres. Bronx

Zoo exhibit designer Walter Deichmann knew this when he was assigned to develop an underground city for naked mole-rats. Unlike any exhibit in existence, this was to house both the colony headed by the mole-rat queen Mary and another colony in an attached but separate compartment. The size of the exhibit would be fifteen feet long, six to seven feet across, and three to four feet deep, and within that small space Walter would have to create a subterranean metropolis of awesome complexity.

Before Walter became involved, mole-rat exhibits were rather like the ant farms that some people keep in their homes to watch the bustling underground activities of these insects. Most common were cutaways of mole-rat tunnels visible against a flat pane of glass, but the Mammal Department wanted to present a three-dimensional view of the whole mole-rat colony. Walter wanted people who saw it to feel like they were looking deep underground, into the tunnels, chambers, and mysterious nooks and crannies of this subterranean world, while glimpsing the second colony in the distance.

Walter had to come up with some pretty ingenious architecture, but he also had to cope with some very special problems. The exhibit was to be built in the zoo's World of Darkness, a building with an interior that had to be visible to people while being lit only dimly. Also, mole-rats love to burrow, and their tusks can chew through everything—even concrete—so Walter had to make sure his materials were moleproof. mole-rats are also supersensitive to sudden sounds and vibrations, which would be hard to combat with hundreds of people walking by every day.

When the exhibit finally opened, it was a spectacular sight. Visitors were able to watch mole-rats creep through a maze of tunnels softly illuminated by fiber optics. Although mole-rats are accustomed to absolute darkness, their eyes are so tiny that they couldn't see the soft light, so it didn't bother them. Surrounding the tunnels was what appeared to be the hard-packed soil of East African deserts. And though it was hard, all right, it wasn't actually soil. Walter had created it out of heavy-duty concrete-like material. The mole-rats occasionally gnaw on it, but the keepers have a regular supply on hand and dab it on when the mole-rats cause too much damage.

Some of the tunnels face toward the rear of the exhibit. You might think that this would block the mole-rats from view, but mirrors have been placed at the back of the exhibit so the images of the mole-rats in the rear-facing tunnels are reflected forward. Two television monitors allow visitors to see close-up views of the colony's inhabitants on "mole cams." One of the monitors even identifies the name, birth date, sex, and social class of certain mole-rats that appear. These mole-rats have tiny electronic sensors implanted under their baggy skin that can be picked up by the monitoring equipment.

To keep the mole-rats undisturbed by sudden noises from the outside, Walter soundproofed the exhibit, much as a recording studio is kept free of exterior noise. He also installed tiny speakers that continuously pipe recorded music into the tunnels. Just like some kids get used to doing their homework while listening to music, the mole-rats quickly became accustomed to the background noise, and it helped block out any sounds that might frighten them. Also, to keep vibrations at a minimum, the exhibit is not firmly attached to the walls or the floor, and it is encased in rubber to cushion it from the footfalls of people walking by or even bumping into the viewing glass. As to the type of music that the mole-rats listen to, "it's Bach or rock 'n' roll, it makes no difference," say the keepers.

The exhibit was an immediate success, largely due to Walter's imagination, but "designing it took a flight of fancy," he says. Those involved in planning the exhibit did their best to make it easy for keepers to care for the exhibit. Magnetic strips attach the front glass panel so it can be easily removed, and the tunnels are built in sections, each of which can be sealed off with sliding panels. These panels are just miniature versions of the large sliding doors used to seal off portions of exhibits that house big animals, such as tigers and bears. The effort put into the naked mole-rat exhibit shows that the zoo is just as interested in teaching people about small, little-known creatures as it is with big, glamorous animals. ■

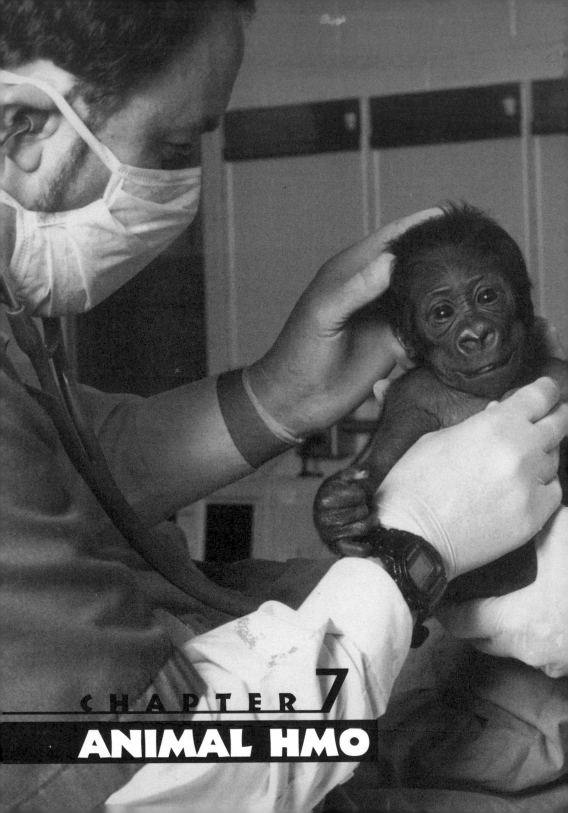

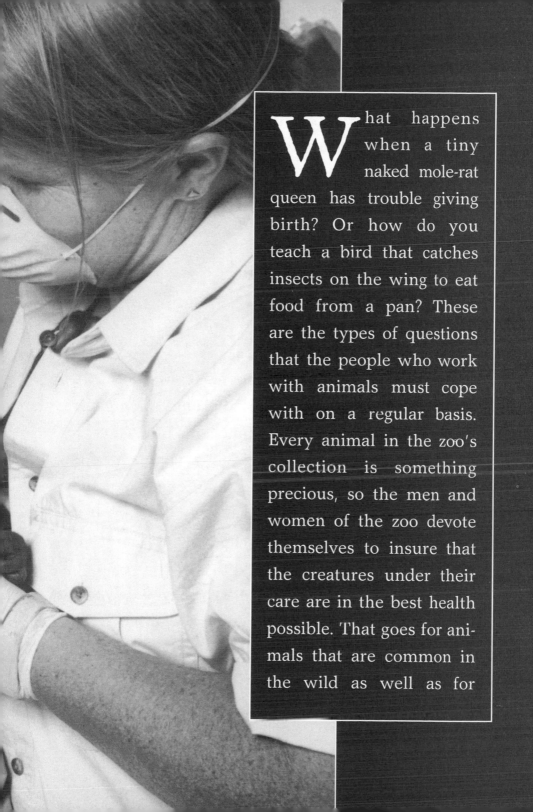

What happens when a tiny naked mole-rat queen has trouble giving birth? Or how do you teach a bird that catches insects on the wing to eat food from a pan? These are the types of questions that the people who work with animals must cope with on a regular basis. Every animal in the zoo's collection is something precious, so the men and women of the zoo devote themselves to insure that the creatures under their care are in the best health possible. That goes for animals that are common in the wild as well as for

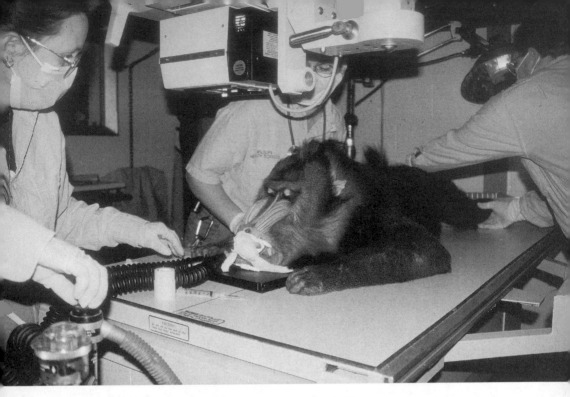

those that are rare. It makes no difference if a creature is as big and spectacular as a rhinoceros or as small as a frog, the animals at the Bronx Zoo have much better chances of surviving and living long lives than they would in the wild. They receive continual care from some of the finest and most experienced animal health experts in the world. Along with the zoo's animal departments, its Wildlife Health Sciences Division, headquartered in the modern Wildlife Health Sciences Center, is responsible for keeping the bevy of animals in the Bronx in top health and, in case of problems, **for providing the best veterinary care possible.** The division also cares for animals at the Wildlife Conservation Society's three other zoos and aquarium in New York City and a wildlife breeding center in Georgia. The division staffers totally dedicate themselves to their job. "Maintaining the health of the wildlife we hold in trust is crucial to their survival," says Dr. Bob Cook, chief veterinarian and director of the division.

The Wildlife Health Sciences Center at the zoo resembles a hospital for humans in many ways. It has a spanking clean operating room, examination rooms,

and laboratories. Instead of bedrooms for its patients, however, the center has cages. Animals stay in these cages when they are **recovering from illness or injury,** or when they first arrive at the zoo. When grizzly bears Archie, Jughead, Betty, and Veronica came to the zoo, for instance, their first weeks were spent at the center under careful watch of veterinarians and technicians.

## Zoo Doctors

From day to day Dr. Bob Cook and his veterinarians never know what they will come up against. They have performed a root canal on a polar bear and repaired a tiger's broken tooth. And once another polar bear, a cub named Tundra, was found with a broken leg and toes. Pins were placed in his leg to repair it, and his toes were placed in a cast. It was changed weekly for twelve weeks, and after that Tundra was nearly as good as new.

Although emergencies occur, says Bob, **"most of what we do is preventive medicine."** The zoo has an ongoing vaccination program to safeguard animals from preventable diseases. **Gazelles,** Bob notes, are among the most difficult animals to vaccinate, because they spook very easily, so they have to be treated with extreme gentleness and calmness.

Everyone who works with animals at the zoo keeps a constant eye out for health problems, but

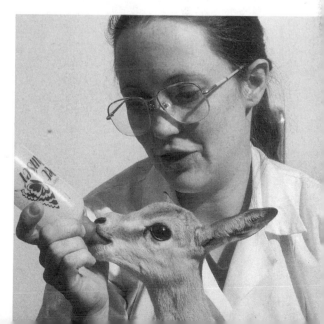

it is not always easy to tell that an animal is hurt or sick. "Wild animals tend to hide their problems," says Bob. "So you have to learn the signs of trouble, and our wildlife health staff can't keep watch over every animal in the zoo all the time. That's the job of keepers.

## SURGICAL SOLUTIONS

Zoo veterinarians have come up with some pretty ingenious solutions that enable them to perform surgery on difficult animals. To penetrate the massive bones of an animal as large as a rhinoceros, for example, they use a carpenter's electric drill modified for veterinary work. Or if a frog has to be anesthetized, it is either placed in a plastic bag full of water mixed with anesthetic or coated with an anesthetic gel. This is because frogs absorb the anesthetic through their skin, just as they do water and oxygen. ◆

They are our eyes and ears, **watching to see if animals appear sluggish or if they are not eating.** These things are usually the first hints that an animal isn't well."

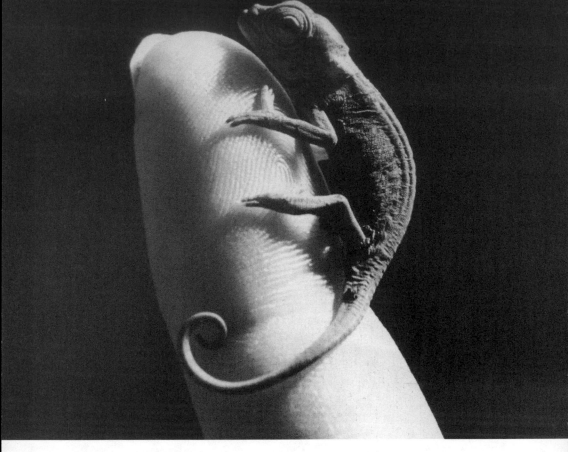

## Microsurgery on Micro Creatures

An alert observation by a curator helped the zoo veterinarians save the life of Mary, queen of the naked mole-rat colony, and her litter of young—and possibly keep the colony from falling apart. Shortly before the Bronx Zoo's naked mole-rat exhibit was to open, Mary prepared to give birth. The colony was being kept in a holding area behind the scenes at the World of Darkness building, where mammal curator Pat Thomas regularly checked on the colony. He had also become the zoo's unofficial expert on naked mole-rats. "I spent lots of time with them, and knew them inside and out," he explains. And knowing that Mary was pregnant, he kept an extra close eye on her, so when it came time for her to give birth, Pat was there. He watched as Mary began to bring another generation of **naked mole-rats** into the world, her tiny body contracting and relaxing as, one after another, eight pups, each hardly more than an inch long, appeared. Pat looked on approvingly at their tiny pink forms as they snuggled up to their mother.

He waited expectantly for more pups to make their entrance, as he knew that naked mole-rat queens usually produce between fifteen and twenty-five offspring per litter. But as Mary's assembly line production of pups seemed to slow down he started to get worried. Several minutes passed without another birth, and yet Mary still appeared to be very pregnant. "I knew that the queen normally produces the whole litter in a short period of time," says Pat, "so I suspected that something was wrong." Even so, Pat decided to wait a little longer, but when more time elapsed without another birth, Pat

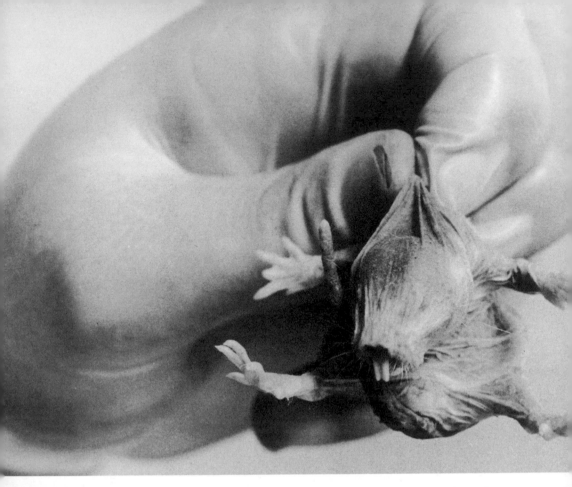

decided to act. He picked up the two-way radio that
many zoo staffers carry and contacted the Wildlife
Health Sciences Center, informing them, "We've got a
problem with Mary. She's having trouble giving birth."
Pat was told to rush Mary to the hospital, located on
the opposite side of the zoo.

**Gently he picked up the little queen,** then
wrapped her in a warm towel. The towel was to insu-

late the hairless little creature from the cool outside temperature. Without the towel her body temperature would have dropped to a dangerous point after only a few minutes' exposure to the air. Carrying his tiny burden, Pat left the building and jumped into the car, turned the key, and headed for the hospital. Bob Cook and his staff were waiting. "It was amazing he could tell so quickly that Mary was in trouble," says Bob about Pat's observations of an animal that was new to the zoo and still puzzling to scientists all over the world.

Once Mary arrived at the hospital, Bob knew that he had to act very quickly, because if a naked mole-rat queen is away from the colony for even a few hours, confusion erupts. Other females try to take over the royal throne, and the newborn young are in danger from lack of care during all the commotion.

Bob and his staff laid Mary on a hot-water bottle to maintain her body temperature, then placed her into a small chamber. They put her to sleep with sedative gas, then x-rayed her to find out what was wrong. The X rays showed that her birth canal was blocked, and to save the young and Mary, Bob knew he would have to remove them surgically. The process that is used when a baby must be removed from its mother's uterus is called a cesarean section, and it is often used when human mothers have problems giving birth. The surgery involves cutting through the mother's abdomen and uterus, then removing the young.

The operation is fairly easy and routine when used on people, as well as animals such as cats, dogs, and horses. But performing it on a creature that is so small it could easily fit in your hand, and is full of inch-long young, was going to be an extremely intricate job. Bob and his staff were going to have to perform micro-surgery on a micro animal.

The cesarean section on Mary was done under a special microscope, and the surgical team opened her up with a laser, making an incision less than an inch long. Using minuscule scalpels and other surgical tools, the zoo doctors made tiny cuts that opened Mary's uterus and birth canal. Ever so gently, with mini tweezers, they removed one pup after another—sixteen in all. Now, with all the pups safely born, Mary's incisions needed closing. Using a microscope, the zoo doctors threaded a minute needle, sewed Mary up, and covered the stitches with a nontoxic glue. Mary and her young were then rushed back to the World of Darkness and returned to the colony. As a result of Bob's quick thinking and Pat's super surgical skills, the colony prospered.

## The Ungrateful Patient

The operation on Mary was very intense for the veterinary staff, but it was over rather quickly. **When animals need long-term care,** however, the staff can sometimes be pushed to exhaustion. This occurred when two baby gorillas—Lucy, a female, and Koga, a

male—came down with an infection of the stomach and intestines. The young apes, each about nine months old and weighing thirty pounds, could not take food or medicine by mouth, so they had to be hooked up to intravenous tubes. This is an easy procedure in human medicine but not on infant gorillas.

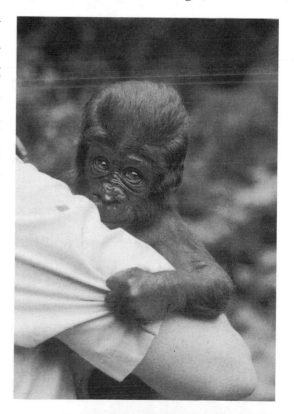

"They try to pull out the tubes or bite them," says Bob. "So we had to be with them around the clock." The health center staff and members of the Mammal Department took turns on eight-hour shifts with the gorillas, and day after day, for almost three weeks, they kept watch. "We were very worried," says Bob. "For the first few days we didn't know whether or not they would survive."

But as more time passed the staff breathed more easily as both Lucy and Koga showed signs of recovery. And then it wasn't long before they were back to drinking infant formula and slurping up ice cubes containing their medicine. The sure sign that the gorillas were back to health came one morning when Bob entered the enclosure with them. Knuckle-walking, Koga approached Bob, who noticed the little gorilla seemed to be in a fighting mood. And he didn't seem a bit grateful for the dedicated care he had received. As Bob watched, Koga stood up and began to beat his chest, acting like a full-grown silverback. Glaring at Bob, the baby gorilla screamed and snorted, but since Bob stood his ground, Koga bit him on the leg. "I gritted my teeth," says Bob, "and happily said, 'They're better, and I'm out of here.'"

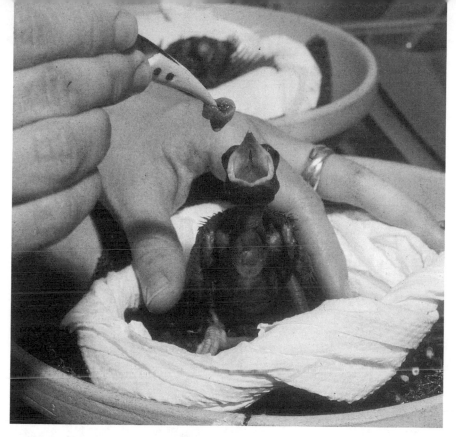

## Many Mouths to Feed

Animals, like people, require a sound diet to stay healthy. Developing the best possible diets for more than six hundred different species of animals is not an easy job. It is often impossible for the zoo to provide animals with exactly the same foods they eat in the wild. There is no way, for example, that a constant supply of fruits eaten by gorillas in Africa can be delivered to the Bronx, the way apples and oranges are dropped off at supermarkets. And elephants, like people, need vitamin E. However, elephants do not absorb this vitamin as effectively as humans, and pound for pound, an elephant must eat much more food containing vitamin E than a person has to to stay nutritionally healthy.

Bronx Zoo curators constantly work to make the diets that their animals receive similar to those they would have in the wild, at least from a nutritional

standpoint, if not the real thing. Luckily, they have expert help doing it. **Dr. Ellen Dierenfeld**, a nutritionist who was hired in 1986 to head the first nutrition department at any zoo, probably knows more about health food for zoo animals than anyone else. Ellen has spent countless hours analyzing animal foods in the laboratory, but she does not stop there. She has traveled around the world examining the foods that animals eat in the wild, receiving information from Wildlife Conservation Society scientists in the field about the types of things that animals eat.

Still, the problem remains that the zoo cannot always supply animals with foods from nature. **"We can't always duplicate what they eat in the wild,"** says Ellen, "but what we try to do is to duplicate the ingredients in those foods."

Apples and oranges, she notes, do not have the same vitamins and minerals as the fruits that gorillas gobble down in the African forest. After some research, though, Ellen found that there was a readily available vegetable that would do the job—the sweet potato. This gave her an idea, so

to solve the problem of elephants not getting enough vitamin E, Ellen turned to **Tus, an Asian elephant at the Bronx Zoo.** As a single vitamin can come in many different forms, Ellen spread different types of vitamin E on bread and fed them to Tus. Consulting with other scientists, Ellen finally figured out what forms of the vitamin were best for elephants, and they are healthier now because of her work.

## High-Fiber Diets

Humans are not the only mammals that need plenty of fiber to have a healthy diet. Many other mammals do too. Without enough fiber these animals may become fat or have stomach troubles. In the wild, lions, tigers, and other big cats consume almost all of their prey, including

bones and hooves, and although these materials are not digestible, they provide fiber. So when Ellen determined that the large "sausages" of ground horse meat being fed to the lions, tigers, and other big cats at the zoo was too soft and causing teeth and gum problems, she figured out the solution: large beef bones, which the cats love to gnaw on.

Another animal that needs lots of fiber is the **spiny little hedgehog.** It feeds on insects, getting fiber from the hard shell, or exoskeleton, that encases an insect's body. Zoo hedgehogs eat cat food, which is nutritious enough but doesn't have much fiber. An insect's exoskeleton is made of a hard material called chiton, and Ellen's research showed that cellulose, which is the main component in the cell walls of plants, has a similar chemical structure to chiton. So now, along with their cat food, Bronx Zoo hedgehogs are fed powdered cellulose.

**Rapunzel, a Sumatran rhinoceros,** once had a

serious problem because she wasn't getting enough fiber. After arriving at the zoo, she developed diarrhea, which lasted for several months, and she was in danger of wasting away. The mammal curators and veterinarians were extremely worried, as they would be about any sick animal, but in the case of Rapunzel, the situation was even worse. Sumatran rhinos have almost vanished from the wild, and only a handful remain in their native southeast Asia, so the loss of even one of them in a zoo would be a disaster.

"We tried all sorts of diets on her," says Ellen, "but none did the trick." So Ellen consulted with Jim Doherty, the zoo's general curator and head of the Mammal Department, who thought about it and came up with an ingenious idea. He realized that, like rhinos, North American moose eat large amounts of sprouts and leaves, and when they do, they also take in small twigs. One of the plants moose feed on is the aspen tree, so Doherty ordered special pellets made from the sawdust of the aspen tree and mixed it with Rapunzel's regular diet, and she quickly recovered. Fat and sassy, she moved to the Cincinnati Zoo, which is one of the few zoos in the world that has an ongoing program for

breeding Sumatran rhinos. She's now back at the Bronx Zoo happier than ever.

Tus, an Asian elephant, wolfs down 150 pounds of hay and grain per day, plus all the apples, carrots, bananas, and treats her keepers give her. Samantha, a reticulated python, eats a pig weighing 30 to 40 pounds every three to four weeks. The **American alligators** each eat two chickens a week, and the marabou storks from Africa get three rats, three horse-meat meatballs, and one trout per day.

## BIG EATERS

Compared with the animals at the Bronx Zoo, the beefy guys of the National Football League might seem like picky eaters. Here's how much chow the animals consume in a year:
* 900 tons of hay
* 357 tons of seeds and pellet food
* 100 tons of fish
* 36 tons of meat
* 4 tons of fruits and vegetables
  [1 ton = 2,000 pounds]

## Ariel's Story

Ellen often teams up with staffers from the animal departments to hatch clever solutions to feeding problems, and few problem feeders have required more head scratching than the carmine bee-eater. The carmine bee-eater is an African bird that catches and eats bees and other insects while in flight. Occasionally these birds are stung by bees, but they have ways of getting around this problem. Once they catch a bee by the wing, they head for a tree. They then whack the insect against the tree until its stinger is disabled. Some scientists believe that bee-eaters even target drone, or male, bees because drones lack stingers.

**Carmine bee-eaters,** as might be expected, are graceful, acrobatic fliers—they have to be to catch insects in midair. They also have beautiful plumage that is mostly a spectacular red color. Producing red plumage takes lots of energy, however, so baby bee-eaters, who must reserve their energy for rapid growth, are brownish pink instead. Few zoos have exhibited carmine bee-eaters because it is almost impossible to supply them with a regular diet of bees and other winged insects. "They really don't react to prepared food," says Chris Sheppard, a curator in the Bird Department. "They want wings and antennae." Carmine bee-eaters also get their red color from chemicals found in insects, called carotenoids. These same chemicals give carrots their orange hue, and on a diet of prepared food adult carmine bee-eaters turn as dull brown as their young.

The beautiful pink plumage of flamingos and the red feathers of scarlet ibises also owe their colors to carotenoids. Both of these birds get the chemicals from the tiny crustaceans on which they feed. Many years ago researchers learned how to duplicate these chemicals, and when they are fed to flamingos and scarlet ibises in captivity, the birds' colors do not fade. One would assume, then, that the carotenoids that keep flamingos and ibises colorful would work on carmine bee-eaters, but this is not the case. So Ellen decided to do some detective work, analyzing the carotenoids in bees and comparing them to those in crustaceans. She found that chemically they were slightly different.

To solve the color problem, Ellen simply had to provide the bee-eaters with the exact carotenoid that they needed. But what about providing the bee-eaters with food? Zoo staffers decided that the best approach was to capture young bee-eaters in the wild and train them to eat food from a pan before they learned to fly. They hoped it would not be too difficult, because after all, when they are still in the nest, young bee-eaters are fed insects by their parents.

Along with a keeper, a young man named Jerry Casadei, who was training to be a curator, headed to the country of Zimbabwe, in southern Africa. They knew that bee-eaters tunnel into cliffs and mud banks to nest away from the hot sun, so the zoo team removed several nestling bee-eaters from their tunnels. While still in Zimbabwe, they fed the nestlings crickets and dog food with tweezers, just as an adult would offer food in its bill, and the little birds reacted well.

Soon it was time to head back to the Bronx, so Jerry placed the nestlings inside an insulated cooler containing a hot-water bottle. The little birds, whose adult feathers had not fully appeared, needed to be kept warm on the long airplane voyage to their new home. Flight attendants were delighted with their small passengers and repeatedly refilled the bottle with hot water. By the time Jerry returned to the zoo, he had not slept for two days, but his work was far from over. Chris Sheppard was waiting, as the nestlings were scheduled to be quarantined for ninety days. There was a huge problem, though—the young birds were no longer nestlings. Their flight feathers had grown in, and they were ready to start flying. "We had not anticipated that," says Chris. "So Jerry and I had to work fast."

Working against time, Chris and Jerry patched together a flight cage out of plastic mesh and bamboo frames, using duct tape to hold it together. "Half the time," says Chris, "the duct tape didn't stick, but we got it finished." The birds were then released into the cage and seemed happy enough, but for Chris and Jerry the long process had just begun. "We were about to become the cleanest people in the world," she says.

Chris and Jerry were assigned to care for the young birds for the three months of quarantine, and just in case the bee-eaters carried disease, Chris and Jerry were also kept in isolation from all other birds in the zoo. To make things even safer, every time they entered the bee-eaters' cage, and every time they left it, Chris and Jerry had to change clothes and shower. So before entering the room where the cage was located, each of them removed their street clothes and showered down. Then after entering the room, they put on coveralls. On the way out the process was reversed. And they had to do this four or five times a day.

But aside from all the showers, now came the difficult part. The young birds still did not know how to feed themselves, and it was the job of Chris and Jerry to teach them. The two anticipated that it would not be an easy task, and Chris, who loves bee-eaters, admits that they "are the most stubborn birds in the universe. Instead of us training them, they tried to train us!"

Chris was right, because young bee-eaters even try to trick their own parents, and when it is time for them to leave the nest, they resist. The parents try to nudge them out, but they continue to act like nestlings, begging for food—they really are clever little devils. Zoo staffers decided to feed the youngsters tiny "omelettes" of egg white, vitamins, and nutrients. At first the birds resisted eating the omelettes from the pan, but they eagerly snapped up tidbits that were tossed into the air. One young female, however, proved to be a fast learner. "She started eating from the pan immediately," says Chris. "And she really seemed to like people." The little bird seemed to enjoy being around people so much that soon she became quite tame. "She would sit on our heads, and screech and chatter."

Chris says that this particular bird is still one of her all-time favorite animals. "Bee-eaters are cool," says Chris. "They are very intelligent birds. But this one just seemed to learn much faster than the others, but that's not surprising. Birds are as different from one another as people are. Some are athletes. Others are bookworms." The young female was eventually given a name that the zoo staffers thought fit her perfectly— Ariel. "If you have ever read *The Tempest*, a play by William Shakespeare, you may know that name. In the play Ariel is a spirit of the air, and our Ariel," says Chris, "is very unusual."

Just as important as nutrition is the manner in which animals eat. Sometimes artificial foods must be

fed in the same way natural items are found in the wild. **Flamingos**, for example, filter tiny aquatic creatures from the water. Inside their boxy, hooked bill are filaments that serve as a filter, and as the flamingo sucks water into its mouth the filaments, like teeth on a comb, strain out the food, which is then swallowed. Since Bronx Zoo flamingos are not fed live food, it is not possible for them to do this. Instead, they eat a soup of bird mash mixed with water from bowl-like feeders. They feed on this mix just as they do in the wild, sweeping their bill from side to side and slurping up the mash.

## Butterfly Bon Appétit

The Bronx Zoo has an exhibit called the Butterfly Zone, which is operated during the warm months of the year and is made of mesh and giant hoops that form a tunnel 170 feet long, 42 feet wide, and 21 feet high. The mesh is off-white, and the tunnel is the shape of a giant caterpillar. Visitors enter the exhibit through the jaws of the caterpillar and walk through gardens of flowering plants where butterflies—a thousand of them—fly free. **The butterflies often land on the noses and heads of visitors** as they pass through.

Within the exhibit butterflies feed on the nectar of flowering plants blooming throughout the exhibit. Although butterflies eat several items, flower nectar is

their main food, so commercial butterfly feeders were installed. The zoo staff thought these shallow plastic dishes, which contain nectar and are topped by a plastic flower to attract butterflies, would be a good way to provide the insects with additional nectar. The butterflies, however, ignored the feeders. After considering the problem, zoo staffers came up with a marvelous idea. They figured out that a brand of plastic mesh scrub pads might provide a solution. **The pads, a bright yellow color that attracts butterflies** like the bloom of a sunflower, were placed in the nectar within the dishes of the feeders. It worked. The butterflies were drawn to the pads, settled on them, slid their long tongues through the mesh, and fed upon the nectar.

## Gorilla Salad Bar

Preparation of meals for many zoo animals begins in the morning, just as it probably does in your school's cafeteria. Many of the buildings in the zoo's animal exhibit areas have kitchens like those in restaurants, full of shiny stainless-steel tables and cutting boards for preparing food on, cupboards, knife racks, sinks, and refrigerators.

At the Congo Gorilla Forest **food preparation for the great apes** begins at about 8:30 a.m. As they are vegetarians, their main diet is a mix of vegetables, like celery, a small amount of fruit, along with monkey biscuits. Gorillas at the Bronx Zoo eat the ape equivalent

of what you might get at a salad bar. A typical gorilla "salad" consists of vitamin-packed veggies such as kale, carrots, celery, and collards. Each adult gorilla also gets a daily banana; the youngsters, a half. These bananas are the way that the gorillas get their extra vitamins—each banana is treated with powdered vitamin E.

The gorillas, of course, love their bananas and come as close as they can to the keepers with their mouths open. Each gorilla tries very hard to make sure it gets its banana ration. "They don't want anybody else to take it away," says Denise Smith. The older gorillas are experienced enough to gobble up their banana quickly, but some of the youngsters will play with their food. And every once in a while an adult may try to take the treat away, so the baby gorillas learn to gobble their banana quickly too.

Odd as it may sound, though, keepers use bananas to help determine if a gorilla is not feeling well. If a gorilla does not eat its banana, there may be something wrong—just like when a pet cat or dog turns up its nose at its favorite food.

The veggie salad is not fed to the gorillas all at once,

but is served throughout the day—in the morning, at noon, in the afternoon, and just before evening. In the wild, gorillas spend most of their waking hours looking for food because the plants that they like to eat are scattered through the forest. Therefore, they eat only a small amount at a time, and one big meal would not be healthy for them. By feeding the gorillas small meals, the zoo duplicates the way they eat in nature. Feeding the gorillas more than once a day also keeps them busy.

Gorillas are primates, the order of mammals to which humans belong, so **they are intelligent, active and curious.** If they do not have something to do, they become bored—and boredom is not good for anyone.

"Gorillas need to exercise their creativity," says Karen Iannuccilli, a senior keeper in the Congo Gorilla Forest. "And we help them do it. One way zookeepers help their gorillas use their brains and hands is by hiding special tidbits of food for them to find." Peanut butter is placed in the cracks of rocks within the exhibit. Birdseed is hidden in hay, and peanuts in piles of pine bark chips. The gorillas actively look for these munchies, which may not be as much of a treat as that morning banana, but are a treat nevertheless.

## You Are What You Eat

There is an old saying, "You are what you eat." This is true, and an animal's place in nature is defined not only by where it lives—but also by what it eats. So by learning about proper diets for animals, zoo staffers both improve the lives of the animals under their care and better understand what they need in the wild—an important step to keeping each and every animal species thriving and well. ∎

# CHAPTER 8

# EXPECT THE UNEXPECTED

Ariel the bee-eater definitely has a neat personality, and her ability to learn so quickly took Chris Sheppard by surprise, but Ariel is not unique among animals at the Bronx Zoo. Like her, some of the other creatures that live there are real characters.

As for surprises, zoo animals are always full of them, and the people who deal with animals at the Bronx Zoo often find themselves in some really wild situations.

## A Pelican Swallowed My Head

Each fall the people of the zoo's Bird Department stage a pelican roundup. It is an annual affair and has been featured many times in newspapers and magazines and on television. The zoo's white pelicans live in a shallow outside pond from spring to fall. However, they must be kept inside during the winter, so when cold weather approaches, **the Bird Department staffers must**

**catch the pelicans** and take them indoors. In order to do this, they pull on high boots so they can wade after the birds, and they herd the pelicans with rowboats. The pelicans cannot fly, of course, because their wing feathers have been clipped, but they can paddle around the water like motorboats. And sometimes, if they do not want to be caught, they can be difficult to corner.

The pelicans that are the most evasive, however, are the younger birds. Pelicans have a very long life span, and the older birds are used to the roundup, having had years of training. Somehow they seem to know they will be taken to a van that will carry them to winter quarters, but even so, it takes lots of slipping, sliding, and splashing—and occasionally falling into the water—to round them all up. Sometimes, even more than that. Not many people know what it must be like for a fish that has just been swallowed by a pelican—but Eric Edler does.

Eric Edler is a Bronx Zoo veteran. He started as a keeper and eventually became manager of the zoo's bird collection. He has had many memorable experiences with animals, but one in particular stands out in his mind: the time that he ended up with his head inside a pelican's pouch.

The pouch of a pelican is made of **flabby, stretchable skin under the lower part of its beak.** Pelicans use their pouch like a net to scoop up the fish that they eat. The pouch can balloon out enough to hold three gallons of water—or in this instance, Eric's head.

It takes a strange situation to end up with your head inside a pelican's pouch, but remember, when you work with animals, expect the unexpected. Patti Cooper, a senior keeper in the Bird Department, was there when Eric ended up headfirst in a pelican's pouch. "It was wild," she says. "And it was really funny."

The roundup started out like any other. Staffers headed into the pond, swishing through the water. The pelicans played their games, and little by little, by hand and with nets, the pelicans were caught. "Get over there," Patti shouted to Eric as he netted a pelican, cradled it in his arms, and brought it ashore. As always, the commotion of the roundup drew the attention of zoo visitors, and they started rooting for the pelicans. Each time a keeper missed a catch, the kids standing by the pondside cheered. But Eric and his people didn't mind that the onlookers were cheering against them; they were used to noisy crowds, and it was their job to get the pelicans inside. After a half hour or so, most of the pelicans had been apprehended, but on an island in the middle of the pond a pair of old birds, male and female, still remained. "They had both been at the zoo about twenty-eight years," says Patti. "So they knew that they had to go to the van."

When Patti and Eric got to the island, they walked up to the male bird, who hardly seemed to notice them. "He's calm," Patti told Eric. "Go easy. You can just pick him up." So Eric moved slowly toward the pelican. The bird looked at him, its eyes unblinking, and when Eric was within arm's reach, he bent down to scoop up the bird. But Eric's foot slipped on a wet rock, and when Eric fell, the pelican somehow opened its beak at exactly the same moment. Suddenly Eric found himself looking at the pelican's pouch—from the inside. "I saw the impression of his face on the pouch," Patti says, laughing. But Eric just reached up, opened the pelican's mouth, and pulled his head out of the pouch. The pelican sure seemed relieved, because after all, what self-respecting pelican would want a human's head in its pouch? A fish, however, would have been welcome.

Today, years after he was swallowed by a pelican, Eric remembers exactly what it was like. "It smelled awful in there."

## Attitude Problem

The pelican that swallowed Eric's head did it by accident, as pelicans are rather peaceable creatures. Owls,

# EGG-CITING NEWS!

Talking about the unexpected, senior bird keeper Patti Cooper once found herself the unexpected mother hen to a clutch of hatchling **black-necked cranes.** Indigenous to Siberia, black-necked cranes are rare. Patti had picked up four crane eggs from an organization in Wisconsin devoted to breeding these and other rare cranes, and her job was to bring the eggs to the Bronx Zoo, where the young were to hatch and be raised.

Patti placed the eggs in a small incubator box, which could be carried aboard a plane. A hot-water bottle kept the eggs warm. The morning she was to leave, Patti got a surprise: One of the eggs started hatching. "I was frantic," she says. Clutching the incubator, Patti boarded the aircraft and sat down in her seat. A flight attendant noticed that Patti seemed worried. "What's the matter?" the attendant asked. Patti explained, and the attendant, who had seen many strange things during her career dealing with aircraft passengers, thought, *Now I've seen it all.*

After landing in Chicago, Patti had to change planes. She lugged the metal incubator, which was small but heavy, toward the gate. A security guard eyed the box suspiciously. "Where did you get that?" he inquired. She told him. He scratched his head and walked away.

Patti boarded the next aircraft and nervously sat down. She repeatedly opened the incubator to see how the eggs were doing. Other passengers couldn't help but notice. "What do you have in there?" they asked. Patti, who was getting tired of answering that question, told them. "They were very concerned," she says.

By then, though, the first crane had hatched and the others were well on their way. Throughout the flight passengers asked her about the welfare of the cranes. "How's the bird?" a lady inquired. "Did they hatch yet?" a man asked. One woman, wanting very much to help, asked, "Can I sing to him?" So, after landing in New York City, Patti made a beeline to the zoo. The cranes, as well as Patti, were safely home, and although Patti might have been a bit flustered, the young cranes did not know it. Nor did they know that they were probably the first birds to have hatched on a commercial airplane while flying over the United States. ♦

however, can be as tough as pit bulls, and there is one owl at the Bronx Zoo that could make any pit bull look

like a pussycat. The keepers in **the Bird Department call her B.A., which stands for Bad Attitude.**

There are few birds fiercer than the great horned owl. This huge bird of North America is so ferocious that it is known as "the tiger of the woods." It gets that description because of its skill as a hunter, and on wings almost five feet long from tip to tip, it glides like a whisper through the night woods, seeking food. Two feet tall, it hunts animals ranging from small mice to creatures as large as muskrats and skunks. Skunk spray, by the way, does not bother the great horned owl. It seizes and kills its prey with its wicked curved talons and tears the flesh of its victim with a sharp, hooked beak. Great horned owls are definitely very tough customers, and B.A. is among the toughest, yet she has earned the respect, and affection, of the keepers who care for her.

B.A. lives in a large flight cage at the zoo's eagle aviary, where she has plenty of room to move around and many branches on which to perch. For much of the day she sits on a branch—as owls do in the wild—and stares at the world with her huge yellow eyes. Keepers must enter the enclosure that is B.A.'s home to clean it and feed her. At any given time it can be an adventure.

Senior keeper Frank Paruolo has dealt with B.A. on a regular basis. He knows that he can never take his eyes off her. "Sometimes," says Frank, "when she saw me coming toward the aviary, she would crouch in a corner. Then, when I entered the cage, she would run at me like an attack dog. I had to be on my toes to keep out of her way."

B.A., says Frank, also likes to decoy keepers into a tight situation. "I think that she likes to put things down so keepers have to pick them up." One day as Frank was cleaning the cage, he noticed that a rat B.A. had killed was, strangely, not eaten. Frank was using the garden rake in his hand to drag the rat from the cage, when B.A. made her move. She grabbed the rake in her hooked beak and held on tight. "She wouldn't let go," says Frank, "even when I yanked it." Frank decided to wait B.A. out, and he put down the rake. After some moments she tired of the game and dropped it. Once B.A. moved away, Frank retrieved the rake and got rid of the rat.

Another senior keeper, Susan Gormaley, has also been involved with B.A. "I don't worry about going in with her," says Susan. "If I can see what she's doing," she adds with a laugh. "I watch her all the time." One day, Susan remembers, she failed to be watchful. B.A. was perched on a branch about ten feet away from Susan as she cleaned the enclosure. "I looked down for one second," says Susan. Before she could look up again, she felt strong, sharp talons hook into her shoulder. "She was there in a flash," says Susan, "sitting on my shoulder and staring me in the face." Susan was not hurt. She was wearing a padded jacket that is used by

keepers who work with large birds of prey. It is protection against claws that can cause serious damage if they hook into a keeper's body. Susan grabbed B.A., pulled her off, and put her down. That ended the confrontation. B.A. had proved her point, and Susan would remember to keep her eyes peeled for B.A. in the future.

Bad Attitude is a tough customer, and any time a keeper goes into her cage, she may attack. No one wants to be cut and clawed by an owl—or for that matter, any animal. But that is a risk that zoo people take. Wild animals can sometimes react in a dangerous fashion. For that matter, so can domestic animals. In fact, more people have been clawed by house cats than by tigers in zoos.

The people of the Bronx Zoo know, however, that they may occasionally be hurt by the animals they care for, and they always remember that their animals are wild, even though they live in a zoo. So even when Bad Attitude seems to be in a good mood, she can always turn into a tiger. That is the way wild animals are, and the Bronx Zoo people respect them for that. It is their way.

**A wild animal is always wild**, even if it has been born in a zoo. It may scratch, bite, and claw, or even— as Eric Edler knows—swallow your head, but zoo animals can also be very caring to the people who care for them. Ariel loves to be near people, and Timmy, who you wouldn't want to wrestle, gently takes grapes and bananas from the hands of his keepers.

A person who works at a zoo lives closer to wild animals than anyone else. They feed them, clean up after them, and help take care of their young. They help them if they are sick or injured, and teach other people about why these animals are so precious. That is their job—and their life.

## Tame but Wild

A small number of the animals at the Bronx Zoo have purposely been tamed **so that people can easily handle them**. These are the animals that are used by instructors in the zoo's Education Department during lectures and demonstrations. You might consider these critters as employees of the zoo, as they help teach people of all ages about wild animals and the need to conserve nature. The Education Department also highlights many domestic animals, such as pigs, goats, and ducks, which can be seen in the Children's Zoo, a mini zoo designed just for kids.

Education Department staffers have some funny stories to tell about their animals. Melissa Wimer is an instructor in the department. She knows that when handling an animal in front of people, you must expect the unexpected. Melissa remembers the time when Parker the kinkajou caused a highly embarrassing moment for a female instructor who was talking to students in a class given at the zoo. Kinkajous, by the way, are tropical relatives of raccoons, although they do not have a mask or a ringed tail. Like raccoons, however, they are very curious about what they see and smell. The instructor

## LIVING CLASSROOMS

When the Bronx Zoo was founded, one of the things that made it different from most other zoos was that part of its mission was "instruction to the public." In other words, people would not come to the zoo only to look at animals, but to learn about them and their place in nature's scheme. In 1929 the zoo took its educational mission to heart. It started the first zoo education program ever. The Wildlife Conservation Society, which operates the zoo, now sponsors environmental education programs in every U.S. state and around the world, as far away from its Bronx headquarters as China. Programs are designed for adults and young people. Other programs teach teachers, explaining how they can better instruct students about the environment, and zoo educators spread the word far and wide by providing publications and other instruction materials to schools and even to national governments. Close to home, though, these educators use their special animals in lectures for people ranging in age from preschoolers to senior citizens. And they use the whole zoo itself as a living classroom. Zillions of school children have been taken on tours of the zoo, where they have learned about subjects such as endangered species and the relationships between animals and the environment. Zoo educators must know lots about animals and nature in general. They must also understand people.                                                    ◆

was holding Parker when he apparently caught a whiff from her armpit. "He poked his nose into the instructor's collar," remembers Melissa, "and dove into her blouse." Turning her back to the class, the instructor removed Parker, whose curiosity had apparently been satisfied, and continued teaching. She may be the only person ever to have had a kinkajou inside her shirt.

## Children's Zoo Characters

The Children's Zoo at the Bronx Zoo is the home of some of the zoo's wackiest animal characters. Take Mama the Llama, for instance. **Llamas,** which come from South America and are domesticated relatives of camels, have a nasty habit. When they are annoyed, they spit, and llama spit is particularly gooey and yucky. Mama apparently does not like her name. When keepers sing "Mama the Llama" to her, "she thinks we are teasing her, and maybe we are," says Alikia Thomas, who works in the Children's Zoo. When Mama has had enough of what she may think of as human

foolishness, she lets loose. Children's Zoo staffers have become very skillful at dodging wads of llama spit. And once you've had a llama spit in your face, you learn to steer clear.

The Children's Zoo at the Bronx Zoo was one of the first. It was opened in 1941. Why have a special zoo for children inside a huge zoo that children enjoy at least as much as adults? **The Children's Zoo is designed to bring children—including those who have little contact with nature—closer to animals** and truly learn about their lifestyles. Learning is supposed to be

great fun. Kid visitors to the Children's Zoo, for example, can climb a twenty-foot-high spiderweb made of rope. While they climb, they learn how spiders construct their webs. They can climb a walkway to a fourteen-foot-high platform, where they have an eye-to-eye view of a porcupine resting while perched at the top of a tree.

And on the floor of the forest they **encounter tortoises** crawling about freely.

One of the most popular areas of the Children's Zoo is for domestic animals. It is the only part of the Bronx Zoo where people can pet and feed the animals. And some of the domestic animals in the Children's Zoo are as full of surprises as their wild relatives.

Merton the goose is one of them. Merton is the unofficial mascot of the Children's Zoo. All day long he struts around, patrolling what he believes is his territory. He honks and waddles, his eyes on everything. Geese are very feisty and courageous. If a goose does not like someone, it will charge, snapping its bill. Even the keepers at the Children's Zoo treat Merton with respect. However, kids have nothing to fear from Merton. When he walks among them, you can almost see a sparkle in his eyes. Merton sometimes acts as if he likes adults—but he *loves* kids.

Among the friskiest creatures at the Children's Zoo are its **African pygmy goats.** They are miniversions of domestic goats and are less than two feet high at the shoulder. African pygmy goats are intelligent and very affectionate toward humans, and some people keep them as pets or raise them for their milk.

The pygmy goats at the Children's Zoo live in a small corral. Because they are so downright cute, visitors love them. And the goats return the favor. They really seem to enjoy the attention of zoo visitors. Frequently the goats become so excited that they cannot contain them-

selves, and they want to mix with the visitors. When this happens, the corral cannot contain the goats either. Over the fence they go, dancing and prancing around the

Children's Zoo, all merry and excited. For the staffers, though, it's roundup time, and they scurry to head the goats off at the pass. But the goats don't mind; to them, it's just a game. When the goats—and the keepers—have had enough exercise, it is back to the corral.

## A Nice Surprise

As pelicans and Mama the Llama demonstrate, the zoo staff must always learn to expect the unexpected. Animals are unpredictable, and that quality helps make zoo work far from routine, at least some of the time. Life at a zoo can be full of surprises, but for the people who work there, it's a wonderful and exciting adventure. ■

# PORTIA

Animals arrive at the Children's Zoo in different ways. Some come from breeders and farms, some are from the Bronx Zoo's own collection, and others go to the Children's Zoo when they are no longer needed for breeding or for exhibit in the larger zoo. Portia, **a ring-tailed lemur,** was transferred to the Children's Zoo from the main zoo. Lemurs are primates, animals that are related to monkeys, apes, and people. They are very primitive and resemble some of the first primates that ever lived, almost sixty million years ago. Lemurs live only on the island of Madagascar, off the southeastern coast of Africa, and they are disappearing because the human population of the island is exploding. The forests in which the lemurs live are being cut for firewood and to make room for farms. The Wildlife Conservation Society is breeding ring-tailed lemurs at a center located on an island off the coast of Georgia, that is dedicated to preserving rare species.

Ring-tailed lemurs live in groups known as troops. The most powerful female in the troop mates with most of the males. The top female in the troop at the Bronx Zoo's breeding station in Georgia was Portia, while others in the troop were her daughters. As Portia aged, however, her daughters rebelled. As they do in the wild, the young females drove her from the troop, so Portia was sent to a new home at the Children's Zoo, where she lives today. ◆

# CHAPTER 9
# GOOD NIGHT, ZOO

The Bronx Zoo's flamingos amble through the shallow water toward their nighttime quarters. They have spent the day outdoors in an exhibit pool. Now, on this summer day, it is late afternoon. The zoo is ready to close. It is time for the flamingos to go indoors, to an enclosure they will enter through sliding doors at the south end of their pool. Visitors who come during the day to watch the flamingos cannot see the enclosure, as it is hidden by a large mound of earth called a birm. When it is time for bed, the flamingos get herded back into their enclosure for the night. The keepers, who wade through the water in tall rubber boots, don't have to do much directing, though, as the long-legged birds have learned the way to their bedroom.

## Bedtime at the Zoo

Across the zoo, in the **World of Birds building**, keepers are pulling down curtains in front of the habitat exhibits. Many exhibits in the World of Birds have no

separators between visitors and birds. Generally, the birds remain in their exhibits to avoid the bright lighting in the visitors' area. At night, however, the exhibit lighting is turned off. So curtains are lowered to keep the birds in their exhibit homes.

In the outdoor Wild Asia exhibit area tigers are retreating into their holding areas, a habit they have learned because that is when they are fed. Black bucks, axis deer, and the remainder of Wild Asia's antelope are also placed in their night quarters, drawn there by food. Even if animals are fed during the day, a treat encourages them to enter their holding areas. In the World of Darkness the exhibit lights go on so that the nocturnal animals can have their "day," and across the zoo, keepers and other staff members are finishing the work of the day and preparing animals for the night.

As visitors file out of the zoo's entrances, most zoo personnel are going home too, but some may remain at the zoo. If an animal is giving birth or a new animal is arriving from elsewhere, for example, staff is always on hand—all night, if necessary. An evening's dinner and a night's sleep are much less important than the welfare of the animals.

## Which Zoo to Choose?

A similar routine goes on at most other zoos through-out the country and, in fact, the world. In New York, though, there are three zoos and one aquarium, all operated by the Wildlife Conservation Society. They are the Central Park Zoo, in Manhattan; the Prospect Park Zoo, in Brooklyn; the Queens Zoo, in Queens; and the New York Aquarium, located near the famed Coney Island boardwalk in Brooklyn.

**THE CENTRAL PARK ZOO** located in the park after which it is named, covers only five and a half acres. It is a small zoo, but its exhibits reflect the world of nature. It has three climatic zones. The Tropic Zone features an indoor rain forest with colobus monkeys and free-flying birds and bats. The Temperate Territory has California sea lions and Japanese snow monkeys that can tolerate temperatures well

below freezing. And the Polar Circle's animals include **polar bears** and penguins, which can be seen from viewing areas both above and below the water level.

**THE PROSPECT PARK ZOO** is specifically geared to children and has more-elaborate exhibits than the Children's Zoo in the Bronx. For example, visitors can walk down a trail in the company of small kangaroos called wallabies, and kids can traverse a marsh by hopping from one giant artificial lily pad to another.

**THE QUEENS ZOO** is based in Flushing Meadows–Corona Park and is devoted to animals of North and South America, which are every bit as fascinating as those from other parts of the world. Here one can see **spectacled bears** from South America, **cougars** that

range from northern Canada to the tip of South America, and American bison and rare Roosevelt elk from the Pacific Northwest.

**THE NEW YORK AQUARIUM** which is the longest-operating aquarium in the United States, is only a short walk from the surf that rolls onto the beaches of Coney Island. This aquatic wonderland is home to marine animals such as beluga whales, sharks, and walrus. Its most spectacular exhibit is perhaps the Sea Cliffs, which is a re-creation of a rugged cliff off the Pacific Coast. This exhibit—which looks, sounds, and smells almost just like the real thing—is home to all sorts of wild seabirds, seals, **sea lions,** and walrus.

## Zoo Without Boundaries

As the Bronx Zoo staff is winding up their work for the day, other Wildlife Conservation Society people are still at work across the world—in different time zones. They are scientists who help developing countries train their own conservation workers and assist in the development of huge reserves for endangered species. They also study the species themselves. For example, in Myanmar, (formerly known as Burma), on the continent of Asia, a scientist is at work training wildlife officers to conserve areas of forest important to creatures such as tigers. And in Mongolia other scientists are studying the status of rare Mongolian gazelles. In the deep African rain forests even more scientists are taking notes on the behavior and eating habits of gorillas and mandrills. Their information is sometimes helpful to the people who work at the Congo Gorilla Forest, right here in the Bronx Zoo.

The Wildlife Conservation Society has more than 150 scientists **working on field projects in more than fifty countries**. Some of these scientists live for years in the countries where they work. Many endure such hardships as extreme weather, primitive living conditions, and the risk of being caught up in foreign conflicts and sometimes war. But their dedication to their work is what helps them persevere.

So when keepers from the Bronx Zoo head home for the night—after their animals have done the same—the sun is rising on other Wildlife Conservation Society workers far from New York City. Perhaps they are studying in a soggy tropical jungle or doing research on a high, freezing plateau in Tibet. Wherever they are, whether it be New York City or Peru, it can be said that the Wildlife Conservation Society works twenty-four-hours a day to preserve wildlife—and that the Bronx Zoo never really sleeps. ■